THE PARADIGM SHIFT

To Anton,
with love

Dec 2011

THE PARADIGM SHIFT

A JOURNEY BEYOND PERCEPTION

D. K. ANDERSON

Publisher
United Media Press

A catalogue record for this book is available
from the British Library

ISBN: 978-0-9576648-3-8

Cover: Earth Winds by Ali Ries

This book is dedicated to all free spirits.

*"If you wish to understand the Universe,
think of energy, frequency and vibration."*

—Nikola Tesla

Prologue

I only met him once, in a bar one winter's night in Nebraska. I was passing through and it was the only place open so late in that part of town. He seemed a little lonely and I needed some company myself that night. Although old, his eyes seemed those of a younger man, with the fine lines of his face suggesting a wealth of experience. He said he used to be an astronaut, an ambitious high-flyer for NASA in the early part of the century, and that his life had changed dramatically over the years because of all that had happened.

The bar had definitely seen better days. It had a dark, down-trodden feel, with one solitary window set high near to the ceiling, allowing an orange streetlight outside to flicker down half-heartedly against the bar wall.

Being just the two of us left in the establishment as the night wore on, he asked if I would like to share some wine with him. I was a beer drinker myself, but somehow it felt appropriate to accept.

A portly barman in a greasy apron brought over a bottle and filled two glasses without a word, before slouching back to watch a television screen behind the bar. The old man said he'd been given many treatments, but this had only enhanced his desire for inner truth and knowledge.

Although I had traveled a great deal that day, the story he told intrigued me so much that when I left, the dawn was breaking over the downtown Lincoln skyline. I never saw him again, but he asked that I tell his story to as many as would listen.

As a writer, I felt compelled to oblige.

1

I stood alone, exhausted, in a hot shimmering desert. A flash of sunlight reflected off the metallic surface of a midnight-blue limousine. A pulsating red light vibrated from the control panel above my head—it was the first indication of warning. People waved, and the president waved back. My feet hurt, as I stood marooned in the hot desert sand. The limousine turned and headed down into the darkness of an underpass. Data scrolled erratically from screens as instruments displayed chaotic readings. Anxious instructions echoed within the chasm of my mind. A piercing scream rang out as flames began to engulf my body.

My eyes opened. I stared upwards at a pure white bedroom ceiling. All was silent. I paused for a moment, and then took a deep breath.

Yes, it all started with a dream, on a hot sultry night two weeks before a key mission. I hadn't paid much attention to dreams before. What were they anyway? Just a bunch of meaningless images produced in the mind to relieve the subconscious of everyday tensions. At least, that was my thinking at the time. But this dream was different, mainly because it had occurred twice before and in exactly the same way.

Dreams were never a part of the Space Agency's training, of course—their sole concern was getting the first American onto the Red Planet. But Suzanne, my young wife, felt decidedly different.

"Why don't you tell Leanchek?" she'd said, the first time I told her. "He needs to know about things like this."

What Leanchek, my flight director at NASA, would have made of it, I wasn't sure. But Suzanne certainly did have strong concerns about this particular mission.

My eyes drifted down to her beautiful body sleeping peacefully beside me. She was all stillness, with moonlight gently flickering across her soft calm face. Recurring images of me alone and exhausted in a desert and Kennedy surviving in Dallas in the sixties wasn't going to stop the launch of course, but they certainly stirred some apprehension within me.

It was six days before the launch. I was walking beside Joseph Leanchek toward his office past throngs of engineers and technicians working on the Space Agency's assembly floor. Leanchek was NASA's Chief Flight Director and coordinator for a classified descent program instigated by the Agency two years previously.

Leanchek was always matter of fact and that day was no exception. Everyone felt a sense of importance in his presence and being on his team was something special. Here was a man very much in charge. After all, he was being groomed to become NASA's Chief Operations Director for Prometheus, the Agency's code-name for the first manned space flight to Mars.

Prometheus was an important goal for everyone who worked at the Agency. We all knew what it meant to be part of that special team. Testing the ability of the new fusion-powered propulsion system to slow a spacecraft for re-entry was an important part of a much bigger mission. This technology was going to provide incredible rocket thrust, which would give us the ability to get to Mars much quicker—weeks instead of months. Foreign governments and intelligence agencies were desperate to get hold of this technology, thus secrecy was very much a part of our operation. But this meeting with Leanchek was unscheduled, and unscheduled meetings were rare just days before a launch.

As we entered his impressive office he gestured for me to sit down in a chair directly opposite him. His highly polished teak desk was completely bare except for a flat metallic display screen and a slim red file with my name, James Holden, printed across the top of it. Although it was quite usual for him to have my personnel file out when we had a meeting, for some reason, it unsettled me somewhat this time.

I sensed the wheels of his mind turning as he swayed gently in his expensive executive chair. Leanchek had worked hard to get where he was, and the Agency, true to their philosophy, always repaid. Thoughts continued to race through my mind, as I wrestled to understand why I was there and why he wanted to see me so urgently.

He scanned my file with a practiced air of thoroughness.

"Only six days to go. Everything okay?" His expression gave nothing away; his voice was calm and level.

"Yeah, I guess we've completed most of the preliminaries."

"Good, good. Any problems anywhere?" Leanchek was always fastidious; any small detail overlooked could, for him, turn into a big event.

My mind raced, seeking anything relevant about the mission I could report, anything he might have expected me to notice. Then, something came to mind. "The boys in the lab tell me there's a lot of solar activity up there at the moment."

Leanchek hesitated, as though surprised. "A little!" he replied, looking up from the file.

I waited for more information, but nothing came. "They say there's twice the amount of activity as there was six months ago."

Leanchek's eyes widened. He put the file down and leaned toward me, resting his arms on his desk. "Does that concern you?" he said, questioningly.

"No, just wondered why, that's all." I tried to match his tone as best I could.

Leanchek leaned back in his chair pondering an answer. The leather creaked as he settled in, taking his time. "We've had some unusual sun-spot activity which could affect a few satellite systems, break up some TV transmissions, that sort of thing."

"Is it serious?"

"It's low level activity, it won't affect our work," he said, dismissively. Any unusual activity involving a highly classified descent program would normally cause at least some debate. I would have questioned further, but I felt Leanchek had another agenda in mind. He'd leaned forward again and resumed reading my file. As I shifted in my chair, I could hear the faint noise of a car outside revving in the parking lot, and thought about driving home later to see Suzanne and the boys. The image calmed me somewhat.

"NVI okay?" he said, still scanning my file.

"It's fine."

They called them Neural Vision Implants—NVIs for short. They were micro vision transmitters and had been placed behind the right eyes of six specially selected astronauts. It was the Agency's new toy, and the results were impressive. Their thinking was that for them to see what astronauts were seeing would give them more data and more overall control. Knowing what we were actually thinking was, of course, not possible. But NVIs were a big step forward.

"Anything else you're concerned about?" Leanchek's expression suggested he wanted to get to the nub of things.

"Nothing that's relevant."

"What about not relevant?"

I desperately tried to figure out what he was really after. I felt he'd have to give me some kind of clue, eventually.

"How's Suzanne?"

That was it. "She's fine," I muttered, trying to sound unconcerned.

He paused and looked at me with deep, piercing eyes. "Sure?"

Leanchek knew his stuff. He hadn't spent three years studying psychology at Princeton to dismiss the mental state of his number one flight specialist. He needed this mission to be a success, and I was aware of the hopelessness of hiding anything from him. I thought about the conversation I'd had that very morning, before I left.

"Suzanne has a feeling this mission is somehow different."

Leanchek's eyes widened with curiosity.

"She thinks there's some additional risk attached."

"Really?"

I'm not sure what aroused his concern about Suzanne. Maybe it was some gossip he had heard, or perhaps one of his gut feelings. Whatever it was, I now realized the precise area he wanted to explore and the real reason for this unscheduled meeting.

We sat in silence for a few moments as he resumed sifting through my file. The noise of the car had gone now. Instead I became acutely aware of every click and hum of the air conditioner, as I waited for him to elaborate.

Finally he set down the file, sat back and looked me in the eye. "Well, if she's that worried, we can always get Neilson to work this one."

I clenched my fist, trying to control my frustration. I felt Leanchek was testing me. "Are you kidding? We're in the final phase of all this. Neilson hasn't worked on all the programs. He's a good flyer, but he's only a back-up man, for God's sake."

Leanchek held his hand up to calm my outburst. In that moment I realized that my position on the project could be in serious jeopardy. What I said in the next few minutes would be crucial. I took a deep breath and sat back in my chair, trying to pull myself back together, to prove to Leanchek that he had nothing to worry about. I adopted a calmer tone.

"Look Joe, we've spent the last two years working our butts off trying to perfect this thing, and we're almost there."

"I understand that. I just don't want it to cause problems between the two of you, that's all."

"There are no problems. It's just that Suzanne can't understand why we're spending time and money continually doing these descents into the ocean. 'Why not feed the starving?' Her words not mine!"

"It's a good argument."

"Okay, maybe it's a good argument—but not when your partner's working on an important mission and doing a job he's damned good at!"

At that moment Leanchek seemed to look into my very soul. He had the power to stop everything I'd worked for—right then and there. One stroke of his pen and I could be back working the day shift.

"Look Joe, I'm fine. Suzanne's mind is highly imaginative. It's what she does—that's why she's such a successful writer."

Suzanne's success as a writer had come early in her life. Before we met she had studied the metaphysical aspects of ancient cultures and developed a unique style of putting these findings into fiction that sold well. We lived very different lives in terms of our work, but it didn't affect our close relationship and we seemed to give each other space when it was needed. Although sometimes critical of the amount of money spent by the Agency, she was supportive and knew it was my life's ambition to succeed in this field.

But at that moment in Leanchek's office, everything felt uneasy. It was as if I were walking a tightrope, all too conscious that someone could cut it somewhere along the line. Normally our training procedures would have ironed out any personal or emotional concern. But Leanchek had taken a personal interest.

"Joe, I just want to complete this thing. It's been a long time for both of us and we're almost there. I understand your concerns, but there are no problems between me and Suzanne. Security will not be compromised."

"Security is not my concern here," he replied. "I'm simply checking on the mental state of my number one flyer before he embarks on an important mission."

He leaned back in his chair and stared out of the window as if in deep contemplation. The silence seemed to go on forever.

Suddenly, his mood changed and the tension was broken. He stood up and stretched his back a little. "Okay, okay. Just covering all the angles, making sure everything fits."

His sudden change of mood took me somewhat by surprise. I hesitantly got to my feet as he walked round the desk and patted me reassuringly on the shoulder. I looked down at my hands as he led me to the door. They were surprisingly steady considering how close I'd just felt to losing everything. This was typical Leanchek. Once he'd made a decision he would immediately move on.

Leanchek's concerns about Suzanne had been resolved, and even if we hadn't discussed my dream it was enough to know I was back on board and ready to complete the mission.

2

Suzanne's parents Sam and Mary were regular visitors to our household. These occasions always brought us together in more ways than one. It gave Sam the opportunity to talk about his early aviation days, and the chance for Suzanne and me to make a few playful jibes at each other.

It was our last meal together before the launch and Sam was in good form, waving his arms in the air, demonstrating his early days as a pilot. Suzanne and her mother Mary looked on admiringly with affection, but only mild interest. After all they had heard these stories many times before.

Our two boys, Chris and Mike, played in an adjoining room in front of the television, blissfully ignorant of the shots being broadcast of floods and devastation caused by the erratic weather conditions prevailing at the time. Occasionally, I would gaze over at the screen, mainly to keep abreast of any new developments regarding conditions at the launch area, which were always a critical factor.

One particular image captured my attention that day. It was of a bright laser beam being projected through blinding, swirling snow. The government had set up an experimental "weather station" in the Arctic region, and it was highly controversial. I had seen the shots before, but seeing it cutting through the streaming snow at night made the image even more dramatic. I remember the eager voice of the newscaster describing how the TV crew had secretly smuggled the pictures out to show the world:

'Many have blamed our extraordinary weather conditions on these Harmonic Laser experiments being undertaken in the Arctic. They see this type of experiment as tampering with nature, something that could eventually get out of control. Other experts say it's more likely to be the unusual levels of solar activity being reported by many scientists and astronomers around the globe. Although the government has refused to comment on these experiments, at least we can now see what is taking place.'

It was controversial, whichever way you looked at it. The dramatic weather conditions were certainly affecting life in the US and many other parts of the world. I remember Suzanne poking me in the side to grab my attention, as Sam was about to stand. I knew, of course, what was coming. Sam never finished a meal without a speech, especially when his son-in-law was about to journey beyond the stratosphere!

Suzanne's mother, sensing the importance Sam attached to these speeches, quickly muted the television, whilst asking the boys to pay attention. They didn't of course, mainly because they had also heard it all before.

Sam looked down at Suzanne and me as he began. "I don't want to make a long speech, but just to say how much pride and happiness you've both given Mary and me over the past years. My daughter a successful writer and a son-in-law—well, it's not every day that a member of our family flies important missions into outer space."

I tried not to cringe as Suzanne squeezed my hand under the table. Before Sam could continue, my secure Agency phone rang. It was time for my departure ... good timing.

Suzanne and I left the house and strolled arm in arm toward my old classic Chevy convertible parked in the driveway. We always left the house together first before a mission—it gave us time to reflect and be together or air any concerns we might have.

"Important mission?" I muttered under my breath. "It's just a test run, for God's sake!"

"It's a bit more than a test run. It's highly classified and it has risks attached."

"We do have fail-safe measures, Suzanne. We're not exactly winging this thing." I would have normally given Suzanne more details except this mission was highly classified. The flight testing of these new fusion generators was vitally important, and if successful, would give us a huge advantage over our rivals. The heat was on, and Suzanne was conscious of this fact.

Before we could continue with our conversation, the boys ran out of the house to make their final farewells. I squeezed them close to me before they ran off to play with our neighbor's friendly dog at the driveway gate.

"Hey, and don't forget my birthday card!" I called back to them.

Suzanne clasped me around the waist and looked warmly into my eyes. "Oh yeah? You think you'll get one, do you?"

"So, what have you got planned while I'm away? Gonna write some masterpiece about the wonders of the universe?"

"And why not? Did you know there are more stars in the universe than there are grains of sand on all the beaches in the world?"

I looked at her admiringly. Suzanne always had myriad facts and quotes stored within her brain.

"So there, I taught you something, Mr. Holden!"

"You teach me everything—except how to fly spaceships."

She jokingly pushed me away, before making an unusual request. "Oh, I want to give you something to take with you."

She took out a crystal from her pocket and placed it in my hand. I looked at it with some curiosity. "What's this?"

"It's a quartz crystal. It was given to me by a shaman—a Navajo elder, when I was doing research work in Sedona. He gave me two; I keep one with me all the time. I've been saving this one to give to you at the right time. He said it connects with 'All That Is'—all the universe."

"So, you're giving me the universe, Suzanne Holden?"

"Not quite, but he said I was meant to have them.

"There are rules, you know, Suzanne."

"I thought you made the rules, James Holden."

I held up the crystal toward the sky and looked at it curiously. "Shaman, eh?"

"Yes, descended from the Anasazi I believe."

"Sounds Russian."

"No, actually, an ancient Pueblo people. Story goes they just disappeared off the planet. Quite suddenly!"

I looked more closely at the crystal. It had an unusual presence about it, as though it was almost calling me to take it. "Okay, but just this one time."

Suzanne smiled back in her usual knowing way. We hugged each other warmly, then I climbed into the waiting Chevy.

"Hey, are they watching us with that thing?" She was pointing toward my right eye—referring to my recently implanted NVI node.

"Only when I'm on the job, honey!"

Suzanne gave me a timeless look that words cannot truly describe. It was a look that seemed to touch the very depths of my being. She knew things that I never quite understood. Suzanne saw the *whole of the moon* and in that moment graciously accepted my crude, playful attempt at wit.

Our eyes continued to meet as I turned on the ignition and revved the engine.

"You take care of yourself," concern rustling in her voice. "And no more of those dreams, okay?"

I never appreciated the poignancy of those last moments as I peered back at Suzanne's fading image in my rear view mirror. I felt her concerns were totally misplaced at the time. I had been trained not to dwell on concerns, but to eliminate them. A sign placed on Leanchek's office wall read: *Always Work for The Eradication of Surprise.* I understood exactly what he meant. Perhaps that's why we got on so well.

But Suzanne's fading image did stir something inside me. It was only later that I would learn about synchronicity and its power and inner meanings, but on that day I had no comprehension of such things.

3

The freedom of the desert was never lost on me. With Carlos Santana's ethereal strings blaring out of my Chevy's speakers, I was experiencing a timeless feeling of freedom. It was the main reason I kept the car for so long—this convertible had always connected me to the sensation of expansion. And that day was no different as I sped along a seemingly never-ending deserted highway.

It was late afternoon when I pulled into Bill Nash's gas station. Nash was an old school buddy who owned a rather run down enterprise just outside a small town. Nash had taken the business over from his elderly parents. He had worked there virtually since leaving high school. It was almost a tradition to stop there before embarking on a mission. Seeing Nash was a grounding experience before moving off into a complex world of computerized algorithms and technical data.

Just like his business, Nash, a portly, mild-mannered man, had seen better days. Although pleasant enough, I'd always sensed an inner frustration in him, as if he wanted to break out and become free somehow.

Nash walked out of the gas station office, took off the cap and started to fill the tank. He generally ran on autopilot when someone arrived for gas, everything routine. In fact, that was a word you could use for most of Nash's life — routine.

"Hear you're going on one of those missions again?" he mumbled, as he continued to fill the tank.

"That's what they tell me, Nash." I got out of the Chevy, walked over to the newspaper stand and flicked through the daily papers.

"Any chance of that free ride you promised?" he called jokingly.

"You're still on my list, Nash!"

"Some chance." he quipped.

I picked up a newspaper and scanned the headline: 'More Floods Expected as Arctic Weather Tests Continue.'

"Never been able to fool you, Nash. That's intelligence!"

"If I had intelligence, I wouldn't be filling up gas tanks everyday."

I put down the newspaper and walked back to the car, looking back at the gas station building.

"Hey, you do pretty well here, don't you?"

"Not the same. You go places. I should have gone into advertising!"

I remember looking at him with some surprise. I had known Nash for quite some time, but never thought of him as having aspirations of working in advertising.

My attention was distracted by flashes of lightning in the distance, illuminating orange-stained clouds beyond a range of distant hills. It was a strange sight, like so many cloud formations and weather conditions that year.

"I had my chances, you know," Nash mumbled.

I turned back to him, realizing he was still talking about the job he had never had. Then I climbed into the Chevy.

"I didn't know that, Nash."

"Need to get out from this place for a while," Nash shouted out over revs of the engine.

"You'll miss the sandstorms, Nash."

We both looked to the steely blue hills in the distance, then to the orange tinted clouds beyond.

"Not those orange ones," he replied, "This goddamn weather's gonna kill us all!"

I looked at him with some sympathy. Here was a man who had wanted a better life, but because of circumstances, was now looking back on what could have been.

It was a strange feeling, leaving Nash alone, isolated in the desert that day. Perhaps I should have sensed a forewarning or some hidden message of what was to come—but I didn't get it.

4

Streams of data reflected off my helmet visor as I lay staring upwards at Suzanne's crystal floating weightlessly above me. I was orbiting two hundred and ten miles above the earth, but at that moment I wasn't focused on any data. Spinning the crystal with my rather cumbersome space glove was mesmerizing. I was captivated by the beautiful streams of sunlight glistening off its smooth translucent surface, reflecting soft spinning triangles of light onto the complex bank of controls surrounding me. It was like being in the center of some cosmic light dance—something I had never experienced before.

But this unusual state of tranquility did not last. I was jolted back to reality by a verbal instruction through my headpiece. A young Spacecraft Communicator at Mission Control was asking me to make an adjustment to one of the retro rockets linked to the new fusion generators. I successfully retrieved the crystal and punched in the new data.

A friend once told me that one's life could change in a moment. He was a bit of a philosopher and I never paid it much attention. But the next series of events or moments within those events were to be the catalyst that would totally change my life forever.

All the procedures relating to the descent had, so far, gone perfectly to plan. I was feeling relatively relaxed, looking up at a small monitor next to my control panel. It was my birthday, and the team in the control center had thought to record an NFL game I had missed due to the launch preparations.

About a half way into the game, an "incoming message" alert appeared on the screen. The NFL game faded, and Suzanne's smiling image appeared.

"Hi, happy birthday!" she said beaming back at me. "The boys found something in the attic. They thought of framing it, as a kind of birthday present!"

She displayed an old faded photograph of me as a youthful looking astronaut during my early training days.

"I was never that young!" I quipped.

"You're right, honey. You were never that young." She jested back.

"How's it all going up there?"

"Okay, I guess. No problem with the weather. Plenty of sunshine up here." It was the best joke I could come up with at the time.

"How's my crystal? Or shouldn't I be asking?"

"Don't worry. I didn't need permission."

"I have the other one, you know."

"What other one?"

"You remember, the shaman from Sedona, he gave me two. He said the two linked together would have special powers."

We continued talking for a few minutes, then a strange silence came between us ... as though time had briefly stood very still and we were stuck in a silent, timeless void, waiting for something to happen.

"Are you okay?" Suzanne asked finally—with some concern in her voice.

"Yeah, yeah. I think so?"

"That was a bit strange," she said softly.

I was distracted by a screen displaying some new alignment data. The information displayed a change in my descent trajectory. Descent co-ordinates were pre-set well in advance and rarely changed. A short burst of technical information was transmitted through my headpiece. I punched in codes to confirm the new alignment.

Suzanne registered my concerns. But, before she could speak, a bright red "visual terminating" caption pulsated over her image. I looked back at her concerned expression as her image froze and then faded from the screen.

A picture of Leanchek at his control console cut in.

"What's the story, Joe?"

"Well, not to put too fine a point on it, that solar activity we discussed, well, its getting stronger than we had calculated."

"You're changing the trajectory at this stage? It's that serious?"

"It's just precautionary. It will cut down on your exposure time and also reduce the chance of damage to the electronics. We'll just be getting data from a different region of the test envelope—we'll be monitoring them from here.

I knew Leanchek was under a lot of pressure to complete the mission successfully, but I knew also that fail-safe procedures were always paramount. I therefore didn't question the decision. What I hadn't realized was that the new descent path was now close to the experimental laser tests being beamed from the Arctic region.

A young radar operator sat watching his screen at the secret government Arctic base station. He was about to finish his night shift when he was momentarily distracted by another screen showing the ionized trace of a laser beam brightly illuminating the dim snow filled sky. Brady was a technical specialist assigned to support the group of scientists working at the station. All the scientists were dedicated to the weather modification program, but the project was highly controversial.

Suddenly, a fast moving object appeared on his radar screen. Brady looked intently at the object, then immediately called his shift supervisor. "Sir, we have an unidentified object approaching our sector!"

5

It was 06:41. I was minutes into my descent when the first moments of re-entry turbulence were felt. It was then that I became aware of unusual vibrations within the capsule. I began to feel some alarm as my instruments juddered and displayed erratic readings. Anxious instructions echoed in my earphones as the vibrations increased. A sudden flash of red warning lights illuminated the control panel. Then a strange orange glow appeared and began to engulf the inner capsule. As the intense vibrations increased, I merged into a blinding, pulsating light. Then I began to lose consciousness as all sounds slowly drifted into the far distance.

When I awoke, I saw the capsule hatch gently swaying above me. I had seen the view many times after other descents—but never after blacking out. There was a strange stillness in the air. Usually, there would have been a constant buzz of radio transmissions confirming all was well — but now there was only silence. The only sound was the occasional sloshing of waves against the capsule. I waited, aware of many thoughts racing through my mind. Perhaps the alignment calculations were wrong or perhaps, because of the urgency of the situation, I had to be brought down far from the recovery ships. Why had I blacked out? I heard the sound of rain beginning to hit the capsule.

Then the storm. Heavy rain beat on the outer surface of the capsule. I swayed violently on the ocean surface, worse than any simulation when pilot training in the early days. Rain battered the capsule with a frightening intensity that was certainly not predicted.

Finally, the storm began to subside. The ocean calmed, I closed my eyes and fell into a deep sleep.

As I opened my eyes I heard the murmuring of the ocean, and felt the motion of the waves caressing the capsule's outer shell. As I listened, I felt concern creeping back in; a tension in my stomach that I could not ignore. I had been waiting far longer than was ever scheduled. Then, I heard the sound of distant helicopters approaching. "At last," I said to myself. "At last." I sensed the sound of human activity outside the capsule.

I squinted upwards as a bright shaft of sunlight hit my eyes. A diver in a wetsuit appeared, silhouetted against the intense daylight. He pulled back the capsule hatch and beckoned me out. I climbed through the hatch and then winched into a waiting helicopter. As I climbed aboard I identified myself using the usual protocol. The pilot and crew said nothing as I was escorted with two other recovery helicopters to a ship located a few miles away. I felt the swirling vibration of chopper blades as the helicopter prepared to land on its weathered flight deck.

My curiosity was first aroused by the strange response of the ship's crew. As I peered through the misted helicopter window, they stood motionless, without expression, staring silently in my direction. Usually, there would have been some signs of celebration on these occasions. After all, they had successfully completed a recovery. But on that day there was nothing except the eerie collective silence.

I was escorted down a narrow corridor by a young officer and then into a large cabin. He smiled at me politely and left.

The cabin had a rather old-fashioned feel about it, dark wooden panels covering most of the walls. It was sparsely furnished with a single bed and a solitary framed photograph fixed on the wall opposite. The civilian clothes laid out for me were slightly oversized. I reasoned that this recovery ship had been assigned late to the mission due to the revised landing location.

I walked over to the framed photo and peered closely at it. It showed a faded picture of President J. F. Kennedy with a general in a tropical setting. Underneath the photo, a small metal plaque was engraved with *Vietnam, Asia 1964.*

The cabin door abruptly opened, and a medical officer entered holding a stethoscope and a medical bag.

"Won't take long. Just routine, sir."

He took some medical items from his bag.

"You took your time," I said, attempting to make conversation.

"That's not my department, sir."

"But you were assigned to pick me up, weren't you?"

"It's really not for me to say, sir."

He rolled up my sleeve and pressed a small syringe into my arm, which drew off some blood.

"What's that for?"

"It's okay. Everything's fine."

The Medical Officer placed a small Band Aid on my arm and glanced sheepishly at me. "Was your mission successful?" he asked tentatively.

I felt slightly uneasy about his probing. "Is *that* your department?"

He looked embarrassed.

"How far are we from base?"

"Not far. We're due home tomorrow."

"Home! What do you mean, home?"

Before he could answer, the cabin door opened, and the junior officer stood in the doorway. "They're ready for that debrief, sir."

I followed the young officer down a narrow corridor and through into a debriefing room. As the door closed I noticed a metal nameplate on the door. It read: *USS Hornet – Conference Room.*

A captain flanked by four naval officers sat behind a long table staring back at me. The captain stood up and shook my hand.

"My name is Captain Muller. I won't make formal introductions. You'll be questioned in more detail later."

I stared back at the four officers, sensing an odd awkwardness in their manner. The captain hesitated, seemingly waiting for me to speak first.

"Can you tell us about your mission?" he finally asked.

I don't know when my suspicions were first aroused. Maybe it was looking at the photo of Kennedy in Vietnam or because of the strange foreign accent of the captain, or even the curious silence of the ship's crew. But the questions they began asking were certainly not routine. I gave them rather vague responses, until I realized they had absolutely no knowledge of the mission at all. "Have you not been informed by Houston?" I asked.

"We're still awaiting verification," replied the captain hesitantly.

My suspicions had been confirmed. For me that was the end of their so called debrief. I stood up abruptly. "I don't know what this debrief's all about, but I'm not saying anything more until I'm flown to a NASA research base. There's one named after two people: Dryden and Armstrong. Do you know this place?"

To my utter surprise, this was met with unanimous approval. "Yes, we are aware of the base, Mr. Holden." the captain replied. "You will be flown by one of our top pilots. Our escort helicopters are standing by."

6

My helicopter pilot was a nice enough guy, mid-twenties and full of enthusiasm.

"Be at the NASA facility in seventy five minutes, sir," he said as we climbed into one of the three helicopters waiting on the flight deck. I felt somewhat bemused at his calm and casual manner and the lack of any security personnel aboard.

As I belted up, I enquired about the two other helicopters which were also preparing to take off.

"Our escorts, sir, it's just routine," he shouted, as the roar of the chopper blades began to gain volume.

We took off and drifted away from the ship. I peered back at the two escort helicopters which were now following us. I looked over at the young pilot, his eyes fully focused ahead, then down at his ID badge which read 'William S Bradley - US Navy.'

"What were your history grades, Bradley?"

"History, sir? Oh, quite good. Why are you asking?"

"I didn't know President Kennedy went to Vietnam?"

"Which President Kennedy are we speaking of, sir?"

I didn't reply to his question.

"Your captain, is he Russian?" My suspicions now heightened.

"No, sir, East German. It's all part of these naval centenary celebrations. He's a part of the international exchange program we're doing."

I peered down through the chopper window at the endless flowing desert below, then I turned to Bradley and shouted over the engine roar. "What's this place called?"

"Sonoran Desert, sir. It has beautiful cacti. I got pretty good grades in geography as well, sir."

I peered once more at the two escort helicopters. They were now flying about a mile ahead. It was time to act.

"Okay Bradley, if you're telling me that's the Sonoran Desert, we'd better go down and check it out!"

Bradley reacted with confusion, not really understanding what I was asking.

I noticed a deserted highway and pointed out to Bradley where I wanted to land.

"I have orders, sir. I can't put you down here."

"I wanna see the beautiful cacti. Take us down."

I reached across and grabbed the throttle stick with both hands, looking hard at Bradley as I did so. I felt the chopper jolt and wobble as he tried and failed to overcome my grip. Realizing the seriousness of my intent, Bradley prepared to land.

The cloud of swirling chopper dust began to clear as I stood silently looking along a deserted highway. Although the sun was hot, a gentle wind softly caressed my face. Bradley sat on a small boulder looking bewildered.

"You'll never get away with this. They'll be back anytime looking for us."

Bradley had landed us, with great expertise, between the huge rocks, unwittingly giving me some camouflage from my pursuers.

As I stood looking along the highway, far in the distance, a silver shimmering object came into view. Shaped out of the shimmering heat, a silver truck slowly materialized. I watched it as it got closer, then turned to Bradley.

"Your people got their facts wrong. The Hornet was an Essex class carrier—decommissioned in 1970. She's a National Landmark and lives in a museum!"

Bradley stared back at me in bewilderment, without comment.

The metallic silver truck finally stopped and waited on the opposite side of the highway.

I turned to Bradley one last time. "I don't know which country trained you Bradley, but you sure know how to fly helicopters."

Bradley stared back with a confused look on his face. I guessed that this was probably the first unsuccessful covert mission he'd been on. I felt some sympathy for the young man. He seemed stunned, but my gut instinct had told me something about the ship just wasn't right.

Dark tinted windows obstructed the view of the driver within as I slowly walked over to the vehicle. The door slid open silently, and a mild-faced man of Native American descent beckoned me in.

7

The first few minutes of our journey were silent except for formal introductions. Normally I would have felt uncomfortable, but on that day it somehow didn't matter. His name was Red Hawk, a kind-faced man in his mid-forties.

"You live around here?" I asked, finally breaking the silence.

"Kind of. What about you?"

I felt I had best give him only as much information as necessary. "I'm a flier. And you?"

"Oh, I oversee things," he replied with a hint of a smile.

It wasn't a particularly revealing answer, but on the other hand, neither was mine. Still, he'd given me his name, and I felt strangely comfortable and kind of safe in his presence. I wasn't sure where I had landed or even where Red Hawk was driving me. I was more concerned with losing my pursuers at the time.

After a while he spoke again. "Red Hawk was also my great grandfather's name. Do you know about our culture?"

I was rather taken aback by his sudden animated conversation. "Not really, but my wife does. She collects those … dream-catcher things."

Again, a quiver of a smile from him.

I had a sudden, overwhelming feeling that I should be honest with the guy. "Look, some people are looking for me right now. It could cause you some trouble."

"Don't worry. They won't find us," he replied calmly.

We must have traveled some seventy miles together without speaking. But, again, for some reason it didn't seem to matter.

A road sign drifted past with the words: 'Hogan Food'.

"You hungry?" Red Hawk asked.

I sat eating some succotash while scanning the strange interior of the Hogan Restaurant. Red Hawk sat silently opposite, watching me. Large cushions were scattered around the room between low tables. The walls were decorated with Native American and ethnic artifacts. The place had an almost hippie, sixties feel about it.

"Not going to eat?" I enquired.

"Not right now."

A few people stared oddly at me, which made me uneasy. "Never been to a place like this before," I said, as my gaze wandered over the unusual décor.

"So, you're not into dreams, Mr. Holden?"

For a moment I wondered which dream he was referring to, before concluding he was relating to dream-catchers. "Not a great deal. I'm an astronaut, Red Hawk. All of my work is based on exact science. Everything has to have logic. Dreams have absolutely no logic."

"Maybe you haven't connected with them yet?"

"You sound like my wife, Red Hawk."

Red Hawk smiled back at me without comment.

A young waitress walked over to our table and gave me a glass of water. She smiled at me but completely ignored Red Hawk, then departed.

"Do they know you here?"

"I'm known around these parts," he replied.

My gaze drifted to a photograph of a sand painting hanging on the wall opposite. It showed a large cavernous volcanic rock rising from golden desert dunes. Above the rock was a swirling saucer like cloud. "What's that?"

Red Hawk looked over at the painting. "It's of one of our sacred sites—part of our ancient heritage. You may get to know such places."

"What are you, Red Hawk, some kind of psychic travel guide?"

"Most people believe the visible surface of Earth is the only surface. We believe there are many other surfaces. This painting represents a hidden 'doorway' to other surfaces."

I stared back at him, trying to comprehend his words, but venturing no further questions. I felt a strange presence, being with Red Hawk. His words were direct, but somehow I received them anything but directly. He spoke to me as though I should have known these things already, as though I needed to peel off some self-protective shields to find the real truth of what he was telling me.

I stared out through the windshield of Red Hawk's truck as miles of highway flowed endlessly in front of us. The dashboard was a rolling metallic surface with no defined details. The engine also had an unusual low humming sound. "Is this truck electric?" I asked.

"Sort of electric." he replied.

I must have fallen asleep, for when I awoke I realized we were entering the heart of a city. The streets looked somewhat familiar, but my mind was still muddled. I knew that above all I needed to contact Leanchek and explain what had happened. Finally, we stopped by a roadside junction near its center.

Red Hawk turned to me and smiled. "Well, this is as far as I go with you for now, Mr. Holden."

I stared out of the window as people passed by. They seemed to be walking faster than usual, or perhaps my mind had slowed somewhat due to the journey. As I turned to Red Hawk I noticed him staring at me.

"Well, you were right, Red Hawk, they never found us."

"Did you think they would?"

"I don't know. The things I've been working on are highly classified. There are a lot of people, like foreign agencies, who would want to get their hands on the technology. Before we met, I thought at first I'd been captured and landed in some foreign country. At least now I know I'm still in America."

Red Hawk stared back at me with a knowing intensity. "Seems you're walking a delicate path, Mr. Holden. Seems you need to take care of yourself."

I smiled back at him, not really comprehending the true meaning of what he was saying.

I departed from Red Hawk in a way that mirrored how we met. In silence. His kind, almost translucent face, acknowledged my departure. As I turned to make a final wave, he was no longer there. The space where his truck had stood was empty. It was like he had not existed at all.

8

As I walked away I had only thee things on my mind—to speak to Leanchek, to explain my actions, and to try to retain my position at the Agency.

I was starting to see that everything I had done since landing could have been completely misconstrued as unprofessional. I was unharmed and on American soil and knew that the decisions I had made, right or wrong, could still potentially cost me my career. In Red Hawk's presence, time had seemed to move at a different pace. Now I felt the urgency of the situation once more.

Finally I came across what looked like a phone booth. As I approached it a glass door silently slid open and then closed behind me. I stared out at the people walking by. Everyone seemed to have an air of confidence and purpose. I still had the feeling of disorientation. It was years since I'd used a phone booth and somehow it looked very different. There was a large screen directly in front of me and it took me a while to figure out the location of the phone and buttons below it. I took a deep breath and raised the receiver. A young female operator faded up on the screen in front of me, her plastic headpiece nestled into bright blonde hair. I stared at her with surprise; she seemed to be looking back at me. "How may I help you, sir?" she said, politely. A green light continually blinked from a lens above the screen that seemed to mesmerize me somehow and add to my disorientation. I could see her bright smile fading slightly as I stared dumbly at the screen. Finally words began to flow, as I asked for a collect call to Joe Leanchek at NASA.

"All calls within the States are free of charge, sir," she informed me brightly. I guessed they must have been running some kind of promotion with these new phone booths.

Saying Leanchek's name sent my mind racing again. I knew his reaction to what I had done was going to be crucial. I also knew any hiccups relating to the progress of the Prometheus project would create huge problems for him and the entire Agency.

I waited as the operator punched in some numbers on a keyboard, her fixed smile remaining as she waited for it to connect. Next thing I saw was the operator disappearing and a slightly older dark-haired woman taking her place. She had an ordered air of efficiency about her with the NASA logo placed in the background. I must have been connected through to Houston. "I understand you want to speak to a Mr. Joseph Leanchek, sir. Can you tell me which department he is?"

"He's Operations Flight Director for the Orion 3 project."

I waited for what seemed like an eternity, while the operator's fingers tapped busily on the keyboard. Finally she stopped and tilted her head towards me. "We don't appear to have anybody of that name listed, sir. We also don't appear to have a project of that name listed, either."

I stared at her image on the screen, struggling to control my emotions. I asked her to check once more, and with a sigh she repeated the tapping, before coming up with the same information.

Before I could reply, the image cut away and a thin pale-faced man who looked to be in his late forties appeared on the screen. "Mr. Holden, you don't know me. My name's Paul Ratton, and I'm in charge here." His voice was calm, with a hint of steel beneath it. He was in an office, I could see that, but nothing I recognized.

"Where's Joe Leanchek?"

Ratton hesitated. "He's not here right now."

"Well, where is he?" my voice now louder.

"We need to talk, Mr. Holden. We need a location so we can bring you in."

That was, perhaps, the first time I felt my control of the situation begin to ebb away. "What do you mean, bring me in?"

"We need that debrief, Mr. Holden. The one you refused to give to the officers on the ship."

"Who are you people? What do you want from me?"

"Just tell us where we can make contact. We know you're in Los Angeles. But we urgently need to talk, Mr. Holden."

I slammed down the phone and took a deep breath. I knew there was only one person who could make sense of all this. I grabbed at the receiver, punched in my home number and waited. After a seemingly eternal silence I got the bleeping sound of an unobtainable number down the line. Below the screen my own home phone number rapidly flashed "unrecognized".

The young blonde operator again faded up on the screen. She looked slightly crestfallen when she saw it was me again.

I swallowed, trying to make my voice as level as possible. It was becoming hot in the booth and I was struggling to connect my thoughts. "I want to speak to my wife, Suzanne Holden. She's definitely at this number."

"I'm sorry, Sir, but as you can see on the screen the number you dialed does not exist."

I felt the first signs of panic entering my body. In line with my training,

I looked at the number on the screen and placed my fingers to touch the digits one by one, to confirm what I had dialed was correct. There was no mistake, it was correct. As the monotone voice of the operator began to repeat her words, I slammed down the phone and stood back.

It was then I realized something very strange was happening to me. Panting for breath, I staggered out of the booth and sat on a low wall next to the sidewalk. I tried to gather myself.

I had been vigorously trained for virtually every type of emergency, but this was something else. I felt they had somehow gotten to me. Whatever techniques they were using, whether drug induced or not, they were certainly very effective.

Taking deep breaths, I struggled to think clearly. I grabbed at a discarded newspaper on the sidewalk next to me and glimpsed the headline: *President Berkley Flies to Cuba for Summit Talks with the Soviets.* Perspiration gathered on my forehead. I dropped the newspaper and slumped down on the sidewalk, clutching my face in both hands. My heart was pounding. I looked around at the people walking past. They seemed differently dressed, as if from a different time. Could they all be somehow involved in this conspiracy? Even the traffic seemed odd with many vehicles looking similar, their engine sounds seeming strangely muted. Whoever these people were, I felt they must have given me some kind of perception-altering drug in their efforts to confuse and control me.

I placed my hands over my face, trying to block out the nightmare occurring around me and whispered to myself. "What have they done ... what have they done to me?"

Then I heard a man's voice call out above me. "Jimmy Holden?"

I looked upwards through the tips of my fingers. A man silhouetted by the bright sun was staring down at me.

"What are you doing down there?" he said.

I peered again, trying to see his face. Then I recognized the profile of Bill Nash, dressed smartly in a suit and tie.

I clambered up, and without stopping, embraced him emotionally. In that moment, a feeling of relief flooded through my whole body.

"Nash, is this really you?" I whispered in his ear.

"Yeah of course. Who do you think it is?"

"They tried to drug me, Bill. Tried to get things out of me ... about the mission." My voice quivered with emotion as I finally let go of him—my body still shaking.

Nash stared back at me, looking perplexed.

"But I didn't tell them anything. I told them nothing, Bill."

He put his arm around my shoulders and patted me reassuringly.

"It's okay, old buddy ... it's okay".

"They almost had me, Bill. They made me feel like I was someone else!"

"Well I can tell you who you are. You're Jimmy Holden, my old school buddy."

"That's right. We're old buddies. We go back a long way." I grinned back at him, feeling an almost hysterical sense of release, sweat trickling from my forehead.

Nash looked around at the crowd gathering around us. "Look, you've had some sort of a shock. I'd better get you back home, old buddy!"

We made our way through the gathering crowd and moved toward his car parked nearby. A bystander called out to Nash, asking if I was okay.

"Sure, sure. He'll be fine. He's just a bit shaken up, that's all."

Although he was making light of the situation to the crowd, he couldn't hide the concern I saw on his face.

9

I sat next to Nash, gazing through the windshield as we moved along the city streets. I could feel my breathing slowing as I relaxed and began to feel more settled.

"Never felt like that before, Nash. It was like being in some confused dream. People acting strange. Like everything was becoming slower."

Nash looked over at me and smiled, as if in reflection. "Slower ... right! Hey, remember that guy Cartwright?"

"Cartwright, yeah! Didn't he teach history?"

"Sure did, but didn't he speak just so goddamn slow?"

"Yeah, sure didn't learn much history from Cartwright."

Darkness began to descend as spots of rain splashed on the windshield.

We must have driven for twenty minutes, talking about our old school days, before it hit me a second time that things weren't what they should be. I was so involved in our conversation I was unaware of the roads Nash was taking. I started to look around; but none of the streets seemed familiar. I also began to wonder why Nash was dressed as he was. I had never seen him dressed in a suit before. The last time I saw Nash wearing a tie was at the last college reunion I attended, and that was quite a few years back. These were nothing like the clothes I usually saw him in at the gas station. "Where are you taking me, Nash?" I asked, in a serious tone.

"I'm taking you home, Jimmy".

I felt a rush of heightened suspicion start to creep up again. I could feel my skin turning cold as the realization grew. Why was he calling me 'Jimmy'? He had never called me that before. Nash had always referred to me as Holden. It was like the reality around me was fragmenting for a second time.

"But I—I don't live in this city."

Nash turned to look at me, with a quizzical frown. Before he could respond, we slowed and turned off through a set of iron gates and pulled up outside a large mansion. The rain began to fall heavily as Nash got out of the car. "Nash!" I yelled after him. Where had he taken me?

"Wait there, Jimmy", he shouted back. "I'll go in and get Debra"

"Who's Debra?" I shouted.

But Nash didn't respond. He was already on his way.

I looked through the car window as streaks of rain created blurred distorted images of Nash talking with a dark-haired woman at the front door. Then they came running over toward the car, their coats over their heads sheltering them from the streaming rain. The dark-haired woman opened my door.

"Jimmy, what are you doing here? When did you get back?"

I stared vacantly at her without replying, as the heavy rain splattered my face.

She turned to Nash. 'Doesn't he know me?'

Nash looked at her curiously but did not reply.

"He never phoned. I thought he was still in Africa on his geology trip."

The rain hit hard on my face as I stared at this woman, stunned and frozen, unable to utter any words.

She moved closer to me. "Jimmy, I'm your wife, Debra. What's happened to you?"

I looked back at her in bewilderment, still unable to speak.

The next thing I was aware of was lying on a couch inside the house. A doctor stood over me holding a small syringe, which he slowly injected into my arm. I remember the hazy image of Debra and Nash standing over me. Their images grew fainter as I slowly drifted off into unconsciousness.

10

I woke the next day with sunlight flickering around me. I stared up at a pure white ceiling and watched tiny specks of light dancing across its surface, then looked around the room. It was a clean, sparse and ordered bedroom.

As I got up from the bed, I felt the soreness in my arm from the previous night's injection. I felt woozy and disorientated. I moved to the window and gazed out over an immaculately kept rooftop terrace with a marble swimming pool and views that extended out high above a hazy city. Everything was precise. Even the towels by the pool were stacked neatly on small tables.

Still drowsy from the sedation, I stepped from the bedroom and tentatively moved down a hallway and into a large, lavishly furnished lounge. The décor was uninspiring but very rich, with full-length windows that overlooked another part of the city. I noticed a framed photograph placed on a small highly polished dark teak table. I picked it up. The woman

Nash had called Debra sat on a sailing yacht staring toward the camera, her expression cold and serious. Almost as though she was unhappy about the photograph being taken.

Then, I heard the sound of a man's voice, with an English accent, behind me.

"Good morning, sir." I turned and saw a tall, thin, gentle-faced man in butler's attire standing in front of me.

"Would you like breakfast now, Mr. Holden?"

I stared back at him, somewhat bewildered.

"Madam thought it would be best if you ate something once you woke."

I placed the photo back on the table, followed him into a large dining room and sat at the end of a long, polished, dark wood table. A young woman entered wearing a maid's uniform and nervously poured coffee from a silver container. Without looking at me, she left hurriedly through a side door.

I looked up at a large painting on the wall opposite. It showed a massive corporate building towering into the sky with the words "The Bowen Corporation" etched into its golden frame.

The thin gentle-faced man re-entered the room and placed some glasses on a side table.

I decided it was time to confront him. "Where is ... the lady?"

"Oh, she had to go out, sir, won't be back for a while."

"What's your name?"

To my surprise, he looked somewhat taken aback. "Why, Porter, sir."

"What do you do?"

"Well, I, look after the family, sir."

"Do you know me, Porter?"

"Why, yes, sir, of course. I've worked for you and the Bowen family for over fifteen years," he replied hesitantly.

"Well, I don't know you Porter. I've never seen you before."
I saw a sudden expression of unease cross his face.

"That's perfectly all right Mr. Holden. You're still in shock.
I understand."

I took a sip of coffee. It was rather bitter—whether it was
in fact bitter, or clouded by circumstance, I didn't know. But
I knew I was in a place I didn't want to be, and for the first
time in my life I felt completely helpless.

"We all thought you were still in Africa, didn't expect you
back so soon."

"What was I doing in Africa?"

"You left suddenly. You said it was something essential you
had to do … To excavate for something important … in a specific
cave I believe." Porter seemed to stumble for the right words.

"Really?"

"For you to leave the geology faculty so suddenly, well,
we were all rather taken aback."

I felt emotions swell within me. "Don't try to confuse me,
Porter. I'm not a geologist. I work for NASA. I'm an astronaut.
I know nothing about goddamn geology. What is this place
anyway? Some sort of sanatorium?"

Porter looked back at me with an expression of deep concern. "But this is your home, sir. I'm sure the doctors will do
everything they can to get you right again."

I pointed to the somewhat grotesque painting of the corporate building opposite.

"Do you work for these people?"

"The Bowen Corporation. Yes, sir. As I said, I've worked
here for many years."

I rubbed my aching arm and stared warily back at him.

"You sound convincing, Porter. But none of you are going
to break me." There was an awkward silence between us
before he walked from the room.

I felt then that I had genuinely somehow hurt the guy's feelings. I assumed that he probably didn't know much of what was really going on anyway.

I wandered aimlessly along the hallway and finally back to my solitary room overlooking the tiled terrace next to the swimming pool. I sat on the bed and searched through my pockets. Yes. I still had Suzanne's crystal to give me comfort.

11

The next few days were interesting. Debra looked at me quite strangely each evening at the dinner table, as though I were someone who had gone completely insane. The doctors had drugged me up so much that, at least for the first few days, she seemed to float about at the other end of the table in an almost ethereal manner. The table servers flitted around and asked me about food, but I made sure I ate only what 'the lady' ate. At least Porter showed signs of sympathy toward me.

The Bowen household exuded great wealth, and looked and felt like something between a gothic mansion and a modern day citadel. It was like it had two personalities. Entering through the elaborate wrought iron gates below you felt heavy from the building's imposing presence, but as you rose upwards through the building it had a lighter and more distinctively modern feel. The swimming pool terrace was set high upon a cliff face—overlooking virtually the entire city.

It was in these upper areas that I was able to relax, away from the heaviness of the family atmosphere.

But the days were tedious, and I had little rapport with the doctors. They did their tests but communicated little. I had surmised that it was all part of their game, to slowly extract information from me, but this point of view was about to change dramatically.

It must have been about a week after my arrival when Porter wheeled me into the lounge after my daily tests. Porter was, as usual, making me feel as comfortable as possible. He had put on the television, which I wasn't really bothered about, but I knew he was only trying to help.

"Is there anything else, sir?"

"Well, you could get me out of here, Porter."

Although not meaning to, I knew I again had hurt him with my remarks.

His manner became a touch more serious. "May I speak honestly with you, sir?"

"Why not? No one else seems to."

Porter moved in front of me, clearing his throat as though he was about to deliver an awkward lecture. "Sir, I know you've always been troubled adapting to this family, their wealth, the way they treat people. Your marriage has always been difficult, but we have always been good friends. You know I would never lie to you, sir."

I looked back at him in amazement but with sympathy for what he was attempting to say. "But you're telling me I'm a geologist married to a woman I've never seen before Porter, can't you understand that? Don't try to tell me there's no conspiracy here."

"Conspiracy?" He looked incredulous.

"Look I'm not saying you're involved, Porter. In fact, you make me feel I should believe you. But I don't know you, this family or why I am here. I just want to get back to my own life—my wife, my children, and my work. Can you understand that?"

Porter stared back at me with an apparent sense of helplessness. As he departed I caught a brief glimpse of his face, crumpled as though holding back some deep emotion. It seemed almost genuine. And yet I was sure, without a shadow of doubt, that I'd never known this man.

I stared blankly back at the television screen. More from a sense of frustration than interest, I picked up the remote and began to click through the channels.

Suddenly, an image flashed past that I recognized. I backed up and saw two men sitting in front of a large backdrop showing a sand painting, in a studio discussion. The sand painting was very similar to the one I had spoken about with Red Hawk in the Hogan Restaurant. A young Native American was being interviewed by an older man. The young man had wild looking hair that seemed slightly incongruous next to the interviewer in his sharp suit and tie. I stared curiously at the screen and watched as the interview unfolded.

"So, tell me something more about these sites," the interviewer said, pointing to the sand painting.

The young man nodded calmly. For a moment I thought I recognized him; then I realized what I was seeing was just the echo of Red Hawk in the dignified, upright way he sat, and the time he took to answer the question. "Our sacred lands established a birthright. A birthright that assures a bond between our people and the earth. A bond that can never be broken. That's why our people have became self-sufficient and flourished; it's the source of our creativity and art. This painting of a sacred site represents both the bonding and the creativity. But art alone cannot show the hidden powers of these places. They exist not on one surface, but on many surfaces. Even your leading physicists are beginning to realize the connection between our ancient teachings and the existence of other dimensions of reality."

"Reality … you mean living realities?" asked the interviewer enthusiastically.

"Yes, *simultaneous realities*. We have always known these things, as a part of our culture and wisdom. Many ancient civilizations have understood this."

"You mean physical realities just like ours?"

"Yes, realities existing now in this space and time but in a different frequency to ours. Only very few are able to see alternate realities, but they exist and are very real."

I looked down at my hands and then at the surrounding room. I could feel a cold sweat on my face and a tightening of panic. I realized the faint, just faint, possibility, that what this young man was speaking about could be true and that I had, somehow, entered a simultaneous parallel reality.

My mind raced to recall recent events. The strange orange glow in the capsule—Nash dressed like a business professional—unable to get through to Leanchek or Suzanne—the recovery ship's crew not knowing who I was—the Bowens thinking I had gone insane. It all seemed to fit, but with great unease within my mind. Could this be actually happening to me? I paused the television and looked again at the walls and my surroundings. If this was true and I had entered a different reality, I needed proof. I needed to be convinced and the only person I felt I could trust was Porter. I called out his name, my voice heightened. He entered the room and looked at me, obviously confounded by my sudden animation. I grabbed him by the arm and pointed to the TV screen with a nervous gesture.

"Porter, I need to find out about this."

"About what, sir?" he said confused, looking at the frozen image of the sand painting on the screen.

I gripped his arm firmly and looked directly into his eyes. "I need you to be very honest with me, Porter. I want you to answer a very important question."

"Yes, of course sir. Anything."

I knew that the answer Porter was about to give could be devastating. I took a deep breath.

"What happened on September 11th, 2001 ... 9/11?"

Porter hesitated, and a confused expression gathered over his face. "Was that a significant date, sir?"

"Just tell me what happened on that day, Porter!"

"I really don't know, sir. Was it something important?"

I breathed deeply in an attempt to calm myself. "The collapse of the twin towers in New York City. Please tell me what you know."

Porter looked at me, clearly trying to fathom my questions. "I've never heard of these twin towers sir ... and I know New York well."

"Then tell me about Kennedy, President Kennedy and what happened in Dallas?"

"Which President Kennedy are you referring to, sir? Robert Kennedy or John Kennedy?"

I gazed at him, almost unable to speak. "Are you telling me that Robert Kennedy became president of the United States?"

"Why, of course, sir."

"What year was that?"

Porter hesitated for a brief moment. "It was quite a long time ago ... but I believe it was maybe in nineteen sixty eight or sixty nine. He took over from his brother, John."

I stood there motionless, dismayed, staring at him. I knew Porter was being totally honest. The man standing in front of me was living in a different dimension, and I, for some reason, was also in his dimension.

Suddenly, everything that had gone on before slipped into place. There was no conspiracy. The officers on the Hornet hadn't had a clue who I was. In fact, the Hornet was never decommissioned in this reality. Debra was really my wife, and I was a part of this oil-rich wealthy family. I also realized why Nash had seemed so different. In this world he had made different choices. He had never worked in a gas station but chose to do something totally different with his life.

It all fitted together. I had, somehow, entered a simultaneous parallel reality. I let go of Porter's arm and felt very alone and very scared.

My gaze drifted, through the window, toward the hazy city below. A city that housed millions of people, whose lives had evolved very differently because of the events that had happened in this world.

Then, I became very calm, almost serene. As though, in that moment, I knew exactly what I had to do. I turned back to Porter.

"I am going to need your help, Porter." I said softly.

"Yes, of course," he replied with great concern in his voice. "But may I ask if you're okay, sir? You don't look well."

I looked back at him, but did not respond directly to his question. My mind was racing ahead. Something inside had given me power and focus. My training had told me that if you travel somewhere, anywhere, there must be a way back. Perhaps I would be able to escape from this nightmare, with the right knowledge. I felt adrenaline surge through me.

"I'm going to need a computer, Porter. I need to research some things on the Internet."

Porter hesitated. "Unfortunately, Mr. Bowen does not allow computers in the house. However, we could always use the City Library; they have extensive research facilities there."

"Fine."

"But, may I ask you just one question, sir?"

"Yes, of course."

"What exactly is the Internet?"

12

The following week I immersed myself in research at the library. This was a vast building mainly made of glass with a futuristic looking escalator that flowed throughout its center to the different departments.

In a tall spacious room lit with huge glass skylights I found a quiet corner away from the bleeps and flashing banks of hi-tech information monitors. There was an ultra-thin touch-screen terminal creatively embedded within a smooth glass table and I was able to scroll through seemingly endless archived documents, many scanned and neatly filed.

I found I had entered a world where America had indeed evolved differently, a world where the two Kennedy assassinations had not taken place. Where Robert Kennedy served two terms and became revered as one of the great American presidents. A president who gave back extensive land rights to the Native American people, helped the poor and instigated lasting peace and co-operation with the Soviets. It was all documented. It was a world where Ronald Reagan, Jimmy Carter and Bill Clinton never became presidents, where the Beatles had stayed together longer and their music had evolved even more creatively. I watched in total disbelief taped recordings of John Lennon undertaking a massive Millennium Peace Tour in the year 2000 and saw footage of John and Bobby Kennedy together at the 1972 Democratic Convention.

The Internet had not been invented. All information was amassed into a huge IBM mainframe computer based in Armonk, New York. Most computers, like these in the library, had a direct link into its data and could freely access all information. All around me were people researching, college students doing assignments, others observing recent works of art. Somehow, being in this public building, surrounded by people in unusual clothes, using gadgets I had never seen before, made this world seem very strange — but also very real. Gradually I was starting to understand the magnitude of what had happened to me.

I spent hours with Porter in the library poring over details of this strange new world. I found out that US involvement in Vietnam had ended in 1965 and that a recent manned mission to Mars had been successful. I viewed many archived newsreels, including shots of New York City, with other buildings standing where the twin towers were supposed to have been built.

I read rave reviews of films directed by James Dean in the sixties and seventies and heard the incredible new music of Jimmy Hendrix and Otis Redding. It was remarkable to see this evidence and the visual recordings of these events. It was as if my eyes were opened to a three-dimensional fantasy. But this was no fantasy, it was real. I could feel, see and touch it. But, above all, I knew I didn't belong here. I had arrived in this world through some strange accident of fate, and my aim now was to find a way back. Something inside me was continually driving me forward, telling me it was possible. I just had to keep searching.

I would return to the vast house and face test after test from the family's private doctors. I walked on lines, stood on one leg, completed perception and reaction tests and answered their questions. Once or twice I lost my temper and tried to tell them the truth, but I quickly learned that this only resulted in sedation for the night, and even more tests the following day. I learned that by remaining quiet and compliant, I could avoid the worst of their investigations, and play the role of a harmless amnesiac. Thankfully, going to the library was considered a helpful activity by the family; I think they hoped that something I might read would trigger my memory. I started a regime of swimming in the pool each morning before we left, marveling at the fact that the water and air around me was different from my world, and yet so similar.

With my strength returning and my mind becoming more stable, I immersed myself in studying things I had never thought of studying before. I was intrigued to understand more of what the young Native American man on the television was speaking about.

I began to research sacred sites and places like Mount Shasta, with its strong Native American connection. I read about Lemuria and other ancient civilizations that pre-dated Atlantis and Easter Island. I studied pictographs and ancient stone carvings. I was consumed by an insatiable appetite to learn as much as I could in the shortest time. I read about the Hopi Indians and their understanding of resonance and the creation of matter from energy, about ancient societies that had a deep understanding of harmony and sacred geometry. How they created dwellings to complement the natural flow of energy around them, and powerful healing centers like small temples placed on natural energy grids around the earth. Some called them nodes or portals. Some, like Red Hawk, called them "doorways". I learned how farmers visited these places with their seeds to vitalize them to produce a greater crop yield. How these civilizations understood and benefitted from morphic fields of energy—something that modern science in my world was only just beginning to understand.

Despite all this fascinating information, I was continually drawn back to the world of modern day physics. Whether it was because of my rigorous training or unrelenting desire for proof, I spent hours studying papers about atoms, quarks, electrons and protons—anything that I could relate to other dimensions of reality. I experienced a strange intense focus, as if my brain was somehow being stretched to accommodate this information.

I studied papers from great physicists like Einstein, Niels Bohr, David Bohm, and the neuroscientist Karl Pribram. They had lived in this parallel world, although many others had not.

There were many other names I didn't recognize, including one controversial physicist called Mathew Zeiss. I learned about 'string theory', the 'many worlds' concept and gravitational leakage.

Again and again I mentally retraced my steps to see if there was something I missed during the descent, something I could connect to that somehow made this happen. But always, at the back of my mind, I had the vision of this other person, James Holden the geologist, working somewhere in the depths of Africa, unaware I was living here in his house, with his family, with his wife—a fugitive from another world.

Yes, I had entered into a mind-blowing scenario, a world where many things had changed and were different. But by some sort of grace, I had grasped my situation and was able to observe it without becoming totally insane.

I had an ally, of course. Porter drove me daily to the library, always varying the route to make sure I wasn't followed. He sat with me for hours helping me and answering questions I had about his world. He probably thought I had gone completely insane at times, but he stayed calm, kind and helpful, never questioning my motives. He sometimes went off and came back with drawings and manuscripts relating to some specific ancient teaching. But my focus always reverted to the theories and discoveries of modern contemporary physicists, which I felt were my only way forward.

One afternoon, after our day at the library, Porter and I decided to take a ride around the city in one of the small eco vehicles. These vehicles were quite astonishing to me. They were electrically powered vehicles with diamond shaped solar panels built into their bodies. Everyone called them *bubbles* because of their similar shape. I was told that they were designed by a brilliant young British inventor and engineer named John Bransen, whose company distributed them to most major cities throughout the world.

These micro-cars were available for hire at various re-charging bays in most of the city districts. They were very popular and extremely economical. They were made of a type of a bluish light metal and ran almost silently. They could be hired by the hour. It was like driving a light, manoeuverable go-kart as I zipped around the parking lot to test my skills. Even Porter let down his usual air of formality, with joyful smiles spreading across his usually passive face. We were like small children playing in grown up cars, the like of which I had never imagined since I was a small boy. They looked so strange moving along the city streets.

As we explored the city I saw things I'd never seen before. We saw people at ATM machines looking into cameras for facial identification. Movie house billboards advertising old movies like David Lean's Masterpiece, *Mutiny on the Bounty*, a movie I knew he'd planned but never made. Billboards displaying Pan Am flights to Cuba and the unusual looking hi-tech phone booths, protruding up like silver bullets from the sidewalks, which Porter informed me later were also used as free information centers.

We filmed part of our journey using a tiny family disc camera. Porter always kept this with him, just in case the Bowen family wanted to record something. I think a part of me hoped secretly that I might one day be able to share the experience with my own boys, both of whom I was missing more and more. I never thought I could find enjoyment trapped in this parallel world, but on that day we did have fun!

13

Because of our late afternoon exploits in the city, I had arrived back late. Dinner had started without me. I gave my apologies and sat down opposite Debra. Henry Bowen and his wife Thelma were also at the dinner table and from the expression on Henry's face I sensed he wanted to get something off his chest.

He had been speaking about some land deal as I was arriving and breaking him off in full flight didn't help matters. The young maid who I recognized from the first day I arrived nervously poured me some wine before hurriedly leaving the room. Perhaps she sensed a certain tension in the air. Debra generally acted with a detached coolness toward me, no doubt acting on the advice of the doctors who continued to take measurements and blood samples from me almost daily, but that evening I sensed frustration eating away at her. Henry continued with his conversation.

"So, as I was saying, it was then that these government agents started snooping around. Special Agent people trying to poke their noses into my affairs. I told my lawyers to get them off my back. Last thing I want is for them to jeopardize this deal."

Henry was about to secure oil rights from some spurious Indian land deal and didn't want any complications, especially from prying government agents. Fortunately, as I was to find out much later, Henry's paranoia about authority's snooping had been unwittingly protecting me.

Once Henry finished his discourse, we continued eating our meal in silence. As the minutes ticked by, I felt an icy tension slowly filling the air.

Finally Debra turned to me with one of her cold piercing glances. "I understand you and Porter have been in the city enjoying yourselves today?"

I looked at her, but didn't reply.

"I think it's good you are going out at last. Maybe we can go out together sometime. I think father would like that."

Henry stopped eating and looked up at me, expecting a reaction, but I didn't give one.

"I expect you would have seen things that helped you remember? Did you see our church?"

"Church?" I questioned.

"Debra, you're not supposed to …" Thelma tried to interrupt, but Debra was having none of it.

"The one where we were married?"

"No, I didn't."

"If you just bothered to look at these things, memories would come back to you wouldn't they?" Debra retorted curtly.

"Perhaps he needs to look harder!" Henry cut in, before he resumed aggressively chewing his food.

After a short silence Debra whispered to Henry, but loud enough for everyone to hear. "Exactly what do you mean, father?"

Henry threw down his napkin. "If you ask me, you don't wait for something to happen; you make it happen! If I had waited all my life for things to happen, we wouldn't all be sitting here today eating all this fine food, now would we?"

I stared back at Henry before gazing over his shoulder at a grim portrait of him sitting at his desk in the Bowen Corporation Boardroom. It seemed to me at the time that the artist had captured his personality perfectly.

"Look, don't think I'm not grateful." I said.

Almost comically, they all stopped eating in unison and stared at me—obviously surprised by my sudden animation.

"I do appreciate what you are all trying to do for me, but I'm just trying to understand what all this is about. Like … like what the hell I'm doing here."

"What do you mean, doing here?" Debra retorted. Her voice was high with emotion that she no longer seemed to be trying to control. "You're here because you're my husband. A man who's been married to me for over fifteen years."

Thelma placed her arm around her daughter, trying to calm her. "Debra, honey, you're not supposed to antagonize him like this. The doctors said …"

"I know what the doctors said! I'm trying to stay calm Mommy, I really am, but it's incredibly difficult. We don't even share the same bedroom anymore." She looked directly over at me—her face colored with seething frustration. "Remembering me isn't too much to ask, is it?"

Henry glared at me, still crunching his food.

"What do you want me to say?" I replied, trying not to offend her feelings.

"Just recognize our life together, that's all. I know it's not been perfect. I know you never really accepted the status you gained from our marriage, but at least you used to acknowledge me and treat me as your wife—not like a complete stranger that you don't know or someone you decided not to remember!"

Henry suddenly cut in. "Well, he'll remember okay at the reunion!"

"What reunion?" I questioned with some surprise.

"It's a party where you'll see your old faculty pals again. A reunion that'll jerk your memory, son, where those faded memories will all come flooding back."

"But I don't like reunions." I replied.

Henry scowled. "Oh, so you don't like reunions, eh? Well, we're going to make sure you'll enjoy this one, boy."

Again, the icy silence returned. I got up from the table and left the three of them sitting together. I made my way down the hallway back to my small solitary bedroom, lay down on the bed and turned out the light.

14

It was early evening, as I recall, when the guests started arriving.
The party was concentrated around the large poolside terrace
overlooking the city. It was a warm night and a group of musi-
cians played on a small stage, attempting to create a relaxed
atmosphere. I was anything but relaxed. I stood next to Debra,
greeting the guests as they arrived, not really knowing who they
were or what response I should give. But, somehow, I was getting through it. With his usual charm and patience, Porter
ushered the guests to their poolside tables. There was a hint of
controlled politeness in the air, as newly arrived guests chatted
quietly with each other. Many were surprised and apparently
honored to be at such a unique gathering. They were, after all,
guests of the Bowens, and that alone conveyed bragging rights.

Guests arrived via an external stone stairwell, which spi-
raled up from the finely graveled drive below. This was the
formal entrance. Only very special guests were invited to enter
through the main door of the house.

As Debra and I continued to greet the line of arriving guests, something happened that shook me to the core. A feeling of turmoil gripped me as I glanced over toward the entrance door. Entering the party was Suzanne, with another man. I felt my face pale with emotion as I attempted to pull myself together. I stared in disbelief as she walked with her partner toward us. She looked stunning, as always, with streaks of her dark hair caressing her soft cheeks.

Debra greeted them in her usual way, unaware of my state of mind. "Jim, you know Frank Webb, your colleague from the geology lab."

I stared back at him, as he casually nodded to me.

"And this, I believe, is Suzanne?" Debra asked Frank.

Frank continued the introduction. "That's right. Suzanne, this is Debra and James Holden. I told you about James."

My gaze was fixed on Suzanne as she shook Debra's hand. When our glances met, she raised her hand to greet me. Without thinking, my hand slowly raised and I gently clasped hers.

"I understand you've been in Africa, Mr. Holden?" she said, with her usual bright inquisitiveness.

I was unable to respond with words as emotion welled within me.

"Well, I hope you can tell me all about it — Frank tells me he always wanted to go."

Frank began to look uncomfortable. "Well, that's not strictly true, Suzanne. I've always preferred to do my research here actually."

Suzanne ignored his snub. "Did you get to Kenya? I understand there are some recent geological finds there."

Somehow, I gathered myself and responded. "No, I never went to Kenya."

"What about South Africa?"

"No, I never went there either—In fact I've never been to Africa."

She stared back at me with that curious questioning look I knew so well.

Debra cut in. "You know my husband has not been well recently. I'm sure we will all catch up with each other during the evening. Please help yourselves to drinks."

As they both walked away Debra's calm demeanor began to fracture.

"What on earth are you playing at? I don't want any more embarrassment. Not tonight!" she seethed, trying to control her emotions.

"I need the bathroom." I mumbled with exasperation.

"What? Right now?"

I turned away without replying and left her to greet the line of new arrivals alone.

I stared at myself in the bathroom mirror as my stomach churned. I had just thrown up and felt dizzy and confused. I splashed my face with water, trying to regain my composure. Of all the experiences I had been through so far, this had been the least expected. I knew I had to continue on this strange journey. What other choice did I have? But at that moment I felt very disoriented, fragile, and alone.

I walked out onto a stone balcony overlooking the party guests and stood next to Porter. He was observing the party and ensuring that everything was in order in his usual quiet efficient manner. We nodded at each other, but did not speak. The pool glowed blue beneath us—the lights from the house reflected like ghostly lanterns from its calm surface. Below us, Henry held court with a group of his business associates, all subserviently nodding their agreement. Henry being Henry was incapable of speaking at most people's normal volume. Although he didn't know it, Porter and I could hear most of his conversation.

"… So, one minute he's over there in some cave trying to uncover artifacts and the meaning of life. Then he's back here telling us he doesn't know who the hell we are. I finally get through to these African people and ask them why he left that god-forsaken place. And do you know what they said? I get some garbled message back trying to convince me—me of all people—that he was still there and never left. Sometimes I think this world's gone completely mad. Know what I mean?"

At least I had some comic relief seeing all his associates nodding their heads in unison, in agreement with the great Henry!

I scanned the party guests to find Suzanne standing in conversation with a small group of people by the pool. She looked up briefly and noticed me staring at her. A look of curiosity crossed her face, but there was no recognition. She continued with her conversation.

I turned to Porter, still observing that all was correct and going to plan. "You see that lady by the pool in the black dress, Porter?"

"That rather beautiful elegant lady? Yes, sir."

"Do you know who she is, Porter?"

"No, but she has a kind face, wouldn't you agree?"

"Yes, I would agree very much with that Porter. Because that lady is my real wife."

15

It was later in the evening, the atmosphere was quieter with small groups of guests engrossed in conversations around the pool. I had hardly spoken to anyone. Even Debra had completely ignored me. I was standing alone, deep in reflection, on a small balcony overlooking the dusk silhouetted city. The lights below began to shimmer like distant stars in the warm evening air.

Then a voice behind me broke the silence. "Hi!"

I turned and saw Suzanne standing in front of me. "Nice party!" she said, holding a glass of red wine in her hand. Somehow I gathered myself together.

"Really?"

"Well, they are all here for you."

"You don't know me, do you?"

"I don't think so. Have we met before?"

"Yes, we have met before."

"When?"

"Oh, another time, another place." It took all my concentration not to reach out and pull her close to me.

"Sounds like a line from a movie" she replied—this was pure Suzanne!

"No. It's simply the truth. We know each other very well." In that moment I wanted to hold her. I wanted us to embrace and comfort each other. Then, I sensed her discomfort.

"I think I'd better get back."

"No, I'm sorry. Please stay. I didn't mean to embarrass you."

She moved away a little, but she stayed.

"Are you feeling better? They say you've been unwell."

"That's true. I have not been well."

"Physical?"

"They say psychological."

"Oh, I am sorry."

"Don't be. There's nothing wrong with me."

She looked at me quizzically. "You work with Frank, don't you … my partner?"

I cringed, looking up toward the twilight sky. "Are you married to Frank?"

"He's my partner."

"Oh."

"You're not going to tell me there's something wrong with that, are you?"

"No, I just can't think of you being with anybody, that's all."

"Why shouldn't I be with someone?"

I looked down at the ground—trying not to offend her.

"I don't think I've ever had a conversation quite like this before" she said, sounding slightly perplexed.

I rubbed the side of my eye, feeling a slight ache from the NVI implant.

"You sure you're okay?" she asked with concern in her voice.

"Yeah, I'm okay. Look, I don't mean to frighten you, and this is not going to mean much to you right now. But something strange has happened to me."

"Like what?"

"You ever had *déjà vu*?"

Suzanne looked surprised. "What, when you feel you've been in the same place before?"

"Yes, like you're with the same people, but their behavior is different. Now, just imagine you are switched into this place and it becomes your reality. Not a dream, but a permanent reality. Would you find that scary?"

"Yes, frankly, I would find that scary."

"Well, that's exactly what has happened to me. I'm in a reality that is not my own." I couldn't bring myself to look at her, to see whether she was laughing or, worse still, pitying me. I stared out over the city. The haze in the air was dissolving as the cool night came on. Without the vehicle fumes of my world, the city grew clear and sharp by night. The mountains in the distance arched across the sky and I could see pinpricks of light appearing in the blackness. Perhaps they were other universes, too. I thought of Suzanne back home and the thought gave me enough strength to turn back towards this same woman.

Suzanne was staring at me intently. She had always had an open mind about things, but perhaps this was going just a little too far—even for her.

"Are you telling me this is what has happened to you?"

"Absolutely."

"How can that be possible?"

"I'm not sure. I was descending in a capsule over the Pacific, re-entering, and something happened ..."

"But you're a geologist, aren't you?"

"No. I'm an astronaut … I work for NASA on the American space program. I don't know anything about geology."

"You fly around in spaceships?" she said jestingly.

"That's exactly what I do!"

"How do I fit in to all this?"

I thought for a moment of trying to put it in some poetic way. A way she would understand. But, deep down I felt I just needed to tell the truth. If she decided to leave, if it was a step too far, so be it. I had nothing left to lose.

"Well, you fit in to all this because—Well, because back in my world, you are my wife."

Suzanne looked at me in astonishment. I shrugged and raised my hands expecting a strong reaction. But instead I saw the beginnings of a curious questioning smile. Only Suzanne could be unfazed by an announcement like this and by someone who was a complete stranger—maybe it was a part of her sixth sense.

"Okay. If I am supposed to be your wife, you must know quite a few things about me, right?"

"Yeah, I know quite a few things about you."

"What's my favorite food?"

"Food? Well that's not easy. You like most food. Probably pasta."

"Actually I do like pasta. What about movie stars?" I tipped my head back and stared up at the fading twilight sky. "Well, you had a soft spot for Johnny Depp at one time."

"Johnny Depp? Never heard of him. Try music!"

"That's easy. Puccini."

"That's good. I do like Puccini."

The mention of music flooded me with memories. Like when we'd first met, just being together, listening to music without a care in the world.

I looked deep into her eyes. "You want me to go further?"

"Why not?"

"You hate country music but you love Balinese Gamelan music. You loathe horror movies and love to recite poetry. You wear a lot of black but really prefer blue. You simply adore ancient Greek literature."

Suzanne seemed taken aback by my knowledge of her. "Anything else?"

"Well, it may start to get a little personal."

"Try me."

"You like to sing Puccini in the shower, and you have a beautiful mole at the top of your right thigh, which you sometimes get a little embarrassed about."

She stared at me, obviously trying to understand how I could possibly know all this about her. "What are you, some kind of cosmic psychic?"

"No, I'm an astronaut. I fly around in spaceships!"

Suzanne squeezed her forehead, as though trying to wake from a strange dream. I gripped the edge of the stone terrace, feeling its warmth beneath my hands. We both looked out into the warm twilight haze. The millions of city lights below were beginning to appear like stars as the colors drained from the sunset. For a moment there was an uncanny silence between us.

"How are Sam and Mary?" I asked.

Suzanne gazed back at me with her mouth open. Her face had turned pale. "How did you know them?"

"Well, how are they?"

Her voice began to quiver. "They're both dead."

A sudden feeling of compassion swept through me as I turned to her.

"It was a stupid accident," she continued. "Coming off a freeway. It was like they were there and gone in one moment.

But how could you have possibly known them? I have never spoken to anyone here about them."

Tears filled her eyes, and we became connected emotionally, as though nothing in the outside world could possibly intrude. I tried to comfort her. "He was a brave man. They were both lovely people."

She looked directly into my eyes. "How could you know that?"

The moment was suddenly broken as Frank appeared and bustled between us. He was merry with drink, holding what looked like an invitation card. "I see you two have finally gotten together." He was slurring slightly and I could see a sheen of sweat on his forehead. He'd evidently been making the most of Henry's generosity.

"Yeah, finally," I said, still looking at Suzanne.

Frank seemed oblivious to the connection between us. He cleared his throat and rocked unsteadily on his heels. "I hear you're doing some quantum research stuff?"

"Yeah, I'm working on some stuff."

"Well, what a coincidence. I've just received an invitation from the Academy of Science this morning and who do you think is speaking?"

I finally turned to Frank and gave him my attention. He was practically quivering with excitement. He beamed at me, as though he had won some kind of jackpot. "Zeiss, and he's giving a lecture right here, tomorrow, at the Academy. I've got three invitations."

I looked at him blankly. "Who's Zeiss?"

Both Frank and Suzanne looked at me in amazement. "Matthew Zeiss." Frank responded. "He's the world's greatest living physicist. Everyone knows Zeiss. It's like someone asking 'who is the president of the United States?'"

I quietly thought to myself—who *is* this president of the United States?

16

I accepted Frank's invitation and the next day arrived at the Academy a little early. Porter knew the location and said he would park outside and wait for me. I had wandered inside and moved through the general bustle of the auditorium to a small waiting area. Frank had told me that he would meet me there. The area had tinted glass windows looking outward toward the forecourt of the building. I peered out through the slightly misted window and saw my friend Porter waiting patiently in the pristine black Bowen Limo. Parked on a side street nearby, I noticed a shimmering silver metallic van.

"Red Hawk" I murmured to myself.

As I breathed onto the glass and rubbed it to see more clearly, a blurred image of a woman appeared reflected in the glass. "Hello again."

I turned and saw Suzanne. We stared at each other for a few moments.

"I thought you were coming with your friend Frank?"

"My friendly partner you mean! No, we arranged to meet inside the lecture hall."

I pointed to a large mounted photo of Matthew Zeiss that hung from the Foyer ceiling. "You interested in all this stuff?"

"A little, I guess. You should find him very interesting. Zeiss speaks passionately about the universe and its vast intelligence. He's an interesting man but very controversial. Do you know of his work?"

"Not really."

"Some call him the 'mad magical physicist'. He was a great disciple of a man called Tesla. Do you know of him?"

"Yes, I know the work of Nikola Tesla"

"I'm sometimes asked to do research on him."

"Who? Tesla?"

"No, Zeiss."

"Do you write?"

"No. I'd like to write, but my job is research. It takes up a lot of my time, but I find it very interesting."

"Try writing. You're a good writer. Take my word for it."

"I'll try to remember that advice."

Again, there were a few moments of silence between us as we both looked around the auditorium. Then she made a typical Suzanne comment. "I found our previous conversation very interesting. Are you really from outer space?"

I smiled back at her, enjoying her jest. Our gazes locked in a deep, almost meditative moment. Suzanne then gently broke the stillness. "I want to ask you something."

"Go ahead."

"It's something very important and personal to me."

"Okay."

"Where did my mother and father meet?"

I understood the pertinence of her question and the vulnerability it might stir. But I also knew I had to be honest with her.

"They met one fall in New Hampshire, at a dance. Your mother always liked talking about it. She said it was the most beautiful fall she ever saw. She always spoke about it to us."

Suzanne stared back at me in astonishment. Again tears swelled in her eyes, and her voice became faint with emotion. "How can you possibly know this? I've never talked about this to anyone round here before. What are you trying to do to me?"

Sensing her distress, I moved closer and gently held her arm.

"Suzanne, I don't mean to upset you. I know this is difficult for you to understand, but I know these things because I know you. You are the woman I am married to in my other world. I just need to get back—just find a way back—then we'll be free of all this."

Suzanne looked up at me, her eyes filled with emotion. I caught the image of us together reflected in the tinted glass window. A poignant moment, almost like a dream. How could all this be happening? How could I be holding this woman I knew so well? Holding her in this other dimension of reality. What did it all mean?

We were suddenly jolted out of the moment by the Academy bell ringing throughout the auditorium. People gathered and moved toward the lecture hall. We walked together, in silence, into the hall.

17

The lecture hall erupted with applause as Doctor Zeiss walked onto the stage. He was a man in his early sixties with longish white flowing hair and rounded glasses that gave him a distinguished presence and conveyed a strong sense of integrity. Frank belatedly joined us, and together we sat looking down on the impressive arena below. I felt Suzanne's presence next to me as Zeiss placed his notes on a lectern and began to speak.

"Good morning. Today, ladies and gentlemen, we are observing our physical universe more than at any other time in our history. Even before our first mission to Mars, our understanding of the universe was very different from what it used to be. We now have the potential to understand truths about the very reality we live in. Research is now showing hard evidence for the existence of other dimensions of time and space not just at the quantum level, but at the level of what we observe - our familiar world."

I felt Suzanne glance towards me, as I watched, absorbed in what Zeiss was saying.

"Our optimism increases daily. Even our dreams are helping us understand the closeness of other worlds. Perhaps a closeness that we all feel in fleeting moments of consciousness in our daily lives. Our understanding has no bounds, the only limits are of our own making. We live in a multi-dimensional universe, and now is the time to further increase our understanding of it."

I don't remember the exact moment during his speech, but there was a point when I realized that Matthew Zeiss, the 'mad magical physicist' was the only person on the planet who could help me get back. His speech spoke of resonance fields where amplified objects could be transported from one place to another. He showed diagrams of his own experiments attempting to prove his highly controversial theories. He spoke of Nikola Tesla and how he was discouraged and blocked from letting the world know about his discovery of free energy and how to use it. In some ways our two worlds weren't that different, but in other ways they were dramatically so.

I'd never attended a lecture like it. The crowds of people pouring from the lecture hall and into the foyer were waving and cheering as he walked briskly with his entourage toward the main exit door of the academy building. I clambered through the crowd, my desperation giving me a speed and strength I'd never experienced before, and ran to confront him before he left the building.

I arrived at the grand entrance door just moments before Zeiss and blocked his exit. I was out of breath but my mind was clear. I knew that this was my one chance to confront him. He stopped in his tracks and stared back at me with questioning eyes, as if not knowing if I was about to pull out a gun or to speak admiringly about his work. Even the security guards stood motionless. It was like the moment had frozen for everyone.

"You're the only one who can help me, doctor."

A security guard moved forward and grabbed me by the arm. "Okay, son, you're out of here."

As I struggled with the guard, Suzanne and Frank arrived, looking embarrassed and confused by what they were seeing.

"You must help me, Doctor," I said again, staring straight at Zeiss. Another guard grabbed hold of me and pulled me farther away from Zeiss.

Zeiss looked back at me with some concern then walked past me toward the door. "You must help me. You're the only one who can get me back!"

Zeiss stopped, turned and looked at me with curiosity. He gestured to the guards to release me and walked back to me.

"Back to where?" he enquired gently.

"To my own world, my own time, where I belong."

The guard cut in. "I think we'd better take him, Doctor Zeiss."

Frank moved toward Zeiss. "I do apologize, Doctor Zeiss; his name's James Holden. He's not been well. He thinks he's an astronaut, but he's really a geologist who works for us here on the faculty. We know him, Doctor. I'm very sorry about this."

Zeiss looked sympathetically back at Frank. "I think you had better take care of your friend. Take him home—he needs rest."

As Zeiss began to turn away toward the exit door, Suzanne abruptly cut in. "No, he doesn't. He doesn't need rest. He needs your help, doctor!"

Frank stared at Suzanne with incredulity. I looked at her, knowing that deep down she did believe me, just as Suzanne, my wife, would have believed me.

Frank seemed to lose control. "What the hell are you talking about? Have you gone completely insane, Suzanne? You know very well who he is. He's James Holden; he works with me!"

Suzanne looked toward Zeiss, who stood motionlessly at the exit door.

"Yes, I believe he is James Holden, Doctor Zeiss, but not the same James Holden everyone thinks he is!"

"She's talking crazy, doctor. She doesn't know him at all. She's never met him before yesterday."

Suzanne glared at Frank. "I don't care what you think." She turned back to Zeiss. "He needs your help, doctor. I don't understand exactly what's going on, but I believe there's truth in what he says. Please give him a chance to talk to you."

Zeiss looked at the three of us for a few moments, clearly weighing the situation. "Well, if he is an astronaut as you say he thinks he is, he must be able to prove it!"

Zeiss moved close to me and looked at me intensely with his steely blue eyes.

"Can you really prove this, Mr. Holden? Can you prove you're an astronaut from another dimension?"

"Yes, I can. I can and will prove that to you, Doctor," I replied calmly.

18

With Zeiss having consented to meet me at his hotel room the next morning, I spent the rest of the afternoon at my familiar spot in the library, reading up on his life and work. I knew that my chance of convincing him rested on me being fully prepared for our meeting. What I found fascinated me.

Zeiss was an outsider, an alternative voice whose work was generally dismissed by the mainstream scientific establishment. But his papers and experiments were impressive, and he had many admirers and followers throughout the world, especially among the young. Zeiss was a sort of celebrity, and his lectures were attended by enthusiastic people hungry to know about his views and latest experiments.

Zeiss's work followed on from the work of Nikola Tesla, a brilliant physicist who had lived in the early part of the last century in both worlds. Tesla was considered by many to be ahead of his time; his work included studies in teleportation. His research was thought to have been used on the infamous naval operation known as the *Philadelphia Experiment* where a US navy ship off Philadelphia seemingly vanished, to simultaneously reappear off the coast of Norfolk, Virginia some three hundred and seventy five miles away.

Tesla's work, during his lifetime, was groundbreaking, but this knowledge was felt too valuable to be shared with the ordinary person at the time. He was continually hounded by the authorities, and many of his inventions were frozen or kept hidden.

Zeiss had studied Tesla's work and developed it further, but unlike Tesla, Zeiss would not be sucked in by the government, the military or any other controlling claws of authority. Passionately independent, he saw authorities as wanting to crush and use his work for their own ends. This led the establishment to become suspicious of him as someone who would not co-operate and play their game.

At a young age Zeiss understood that it was a risky business for scientists to take on new, radical ideas outside the mainstream of academic thinking. He knew it was a good way to put one's academic career on permanent hold. But Zeiss was a free spirit, a brave individual and, unlike Tesla, always found ways to keep his critics at bay. The suspicion of his alternative thinking was especially prevalent among the people who worked in the black ops arena and similar covert agencies. It was one of the reasons he'd set up NesCom, a privately funded science project to look into what Zeiss called "the fabric of reality", and went to considerable lengths to keep its work secret from the authorities. Zeiss had been on the government's radar for some time, mainly because of his views on abuse of authority and the controversial experiments he had been conducting. There was some gossip in the media that he was working for the Soviets or other anti-American organizations, though none of this had ever been proved. But the young had no time for secrecy, and it was mostly the young who supported Zeiss in his work. They loved his free thinking.

19

Zeiss was fastidiously taking notes as I sat opposite him in the study area of his hotel room located directly opposite the conference center. He had been going over my story for over an hour and, to his credit, his interest never wavered.

He put down his pen and looked directly over at me. "So, that was the first time you saw her?"

"Yes, the first time."

"Did you expect to see her at the party?"

"No. The only person I had recognized up to that time was Nash, and he had completely changed."

"In what way?"

"Well, he looked completely different. He told me he was some sort of marketing executive, but the Nash I knew ran a gas station!"

Zeiss took off his glasses and wearily rubbed his eyes. "You see, if I were a psychiatrist, Mr. Holden, I might be tempted to call this a case of schizophrenia."

I looked back at him with some disquiet. I knew if I couldn't get Zeiss to believe me, there were very few who would. I had to convince him somehow. "But you're not a psychiatrist, doctor. You're a physicist searching for truth."

The directness of my comment seemed to move him somewhat. He stared searchingly at me then put his glasses back on and scanned his notes.

"It's an interesting story, Mr. Holden. You're been very articulate, and there is a certain logic to your argument. Still, you cannot explain why and how all this could have happened?"

"No, I can't. I have no idea."

"I'll be frank, Mr. Holden. The chance of these events occurring is remote."

Zeiss looked me steadily in the eye as though trying to gauge the strength of my belief. He fell silent, apparently deep in thought. The silence seemed to last forever.

Then, he raised his pen and pointed it at me. "Tell me more about this project you were working on."

"It was highly classified. We were using totally new technology that relied on nuclear fusion to produce longer rocket thrust. Many wanted this new technology for various reasons. Ours was for Prometheus."

"Prometheus?"

"The code name for NASA's first manned journey to Mars."

"I see," he replied with heightened interest in his voice. "So what exactly happened inside this capsule as you were descending?"

"At first everything seemed to be going to plan. It was during the final descent that things started to go haywire. I lost radio contact with Leanchek."

"Leanchek?"

"My flight controller, also the director of the overall project."
Zeiss nodded.

"Then, a strange shimmering glow began to appear inside
the capsule. Objects became distorted and fragmented. It felt
as if I was being pulled by some vibrating force. The vibration got stronger. It was like I was becoming finer—like I was
becoming diffuse, becoming part of everything. Everything
that had ever existed."

Zeiss stared back at me intensely, as if mesmerized by
what I was telling him.

Another silence ensued, as Zeiss completed his notes.

"Your story is very interesting, Mr. Holden. How is it possible that both your world and this world can be real?"

I knew Zeiss was playing with me a little. I felt I had to
be bolder.

"This is not a game I'm playing doctor. I know you know
about these things. You talked in your lecture about the reality
of other dimensions."

Zeiss seemed somewhat moved by my response. He got
up, walked to the window and stared outwards. "My lectures
are about possibilities, Mr. Holden. What all scientists and
physicists need is ultimate proof, mathematical or empirical.
Only then does theory become a reality."

"Can't you know something is real without proving it?" I
surprised myself with the question. It rang more of Suzanne.

"That, if I may say, Mr. Holden, is a profound philosophi-
cal question." He walked briskly back to his desk and skimmed
through an address book on his table, then he turned back to
me. "Okay. I have a friend and colleague who may be able
to help. He runs a highly respected research department for
our space agency. He has the expertise and the technology to
prove or disprove your credibility. We'll see if our conversation
has been worthwhile, Mr. Holden."

I stared back at him with apprehension and relief. Zeiss may not have been totally convinced of my story, but his interest had been stirred and he was taking me seriously.

20

I lay on a treatment bed in a special observation room, watching lab technicians methodically wire me up to various monitors. My eyes scanned the sophisticated equipment surrounding me as they carefully attached small electrode pads to various parts of my body. I felt one being placed close to the side of my right eye, which set off a slight ache.

Zeiss and Alex Morell, a freelance flight operations consultant, were old buddies. Morell had known Zeiss for many years, both as a friend and in a professional capacity. Zeiss had co-opted Morell to do the research on me.

I could hear them through the intercom as they stood next door in the observation bay. Zeiss was calmly observing the preparations for the tests, while Morell was fully animated about a news story he'd seen on the television channels that morning. "It was all over the networks. This guy was picked up from the middle of the ocean a few weeks back. A navy helicopter landed him in the desert, and he just vanished off the face of the earth. They're calling him the mystery man of the desert."

Zeiss coolly pretended ignorance, as he watched the technicians work. "So they haven't found him yet?"

"Not yet, but it's becoming one hell of a story."

I saw Zeiss's gaze wander toward me, but I didn't respond. Then one of the figures approached Zeiss with a nod. "Right, sir, we're all set." The technician's face was completely shielded by the protective mask, and his voice was muffled.

I lay back and tried to relax. Here I was, in a parallel world, being tested by scientists and technicians who had no idea of the journey I'd been on. As an astronaut I was used to tests and medical evaluations, but this was surely the strangest situation I'd ever found myself in.

Morell and his team had assembled an impressive battery of devices to monitor my physical status including conscious and non-conscious responses to verbal questions. The primary instrument was a giant machine called a magnetoencephalograph for graphically displaying perceptual and cognitive brain processes.

As the big machine began to whirr and beep, I closed my eyes praying that this would finally lead to Zeiss accepting the truth of my story.

21

Leanchek was a perfectionist. He let nothing go that he didn't understand, no matter what it was. My apparent obliteration and burnout had become a catastrophic crisis for him and the entire Space Agency. He had not experienced professional failure of any kind before, and this incident had hit him hard. All agency projects had been put on hold, and even the planned Mars mission was in serious jeopardy. Nothing would move forward until answers were found. He spent days scanning reams of data, searching for reasons for the failure. But of course, he could find nothing.

Leanchek did much of this analyzing in the Agency's flight control room, where he had directed my final descent. In front of him were three large view-screens used for displaying real time information during missions. One would focus on the internal view of the capsule. Another would have shown the launch pad or the ocean where the capsule was to descend. The third view was from the NVI implant, transmitted from the node implant.

I was later to learn of these synchronized events, as they'd unfolded in my world.

It was late in the evening, in the dimly lit control room, while Leanchek was analyzing data, when something unusual happened.

A small burst of static suddenly appeared on the blank NVI view-screen. Leanchek looked toward the screen and noticed a monitor needle quiver slightly. A young technician working nearby also noticed it. Leanchek put his data sheets down and studied the screen.

"Wasn't the NVI transmitter de-activated?" He asked the young technician.

"No, sir. As we had no reference point, we just left it in sleep mode."

Then, another burst of static hit the screen. Again the monitor needle quivered. Leanchek, curious, walked over to the screen.

Something incredible was happening. They were actually starting to receive a transmission from the NVI node implanted behind my right eye. On that day, as I was being tested in the treatment room—incredibly—Leanchek began receiving blurred, distorted images from my parallel world. Of course he had no idea what he was looking at, but he did have the foresight to ring Suzanne to inform her of the situation.

22

Awareness began creeping back, and I wondered how long I'd been asleep. The room was dark, with only the regular flashing of the heart rate monitor next to me illuminating the silent instruments. I was in a recovery room adjacent to the observation bay. It was the period of time that Zeiss had advised me would follow after the rigorous assessment process. I was supposed to alert a nurse when I awoke, but something in a voice I could hear had triggered an alarm instinct. I lay very still, trying to recall where I had heard this man's voice before. I gently craned my neck upwards trying to see through into the now dimly lit observation room. They must have left the intercom on.

I recognized the pale-faced man pacing up and down, talking on some sort of radio system. It was Paul Ratton, the same person who'd spoken to me in the phone booth the first day I'd arrived. The man who'd found my location, and who was trying to "bring me in".

As gently as I could, I rested my head back on the bed and resumed my regular breathing. I was hoping he wouldn't notice any change in the heart monitor, but he was seemingly too absorbed in his conversation.

I'd come across guys like Ratton before; he was a carbon copy of some of the black ops people who observed our training. They were always in the background but we knew they were there. They saw anything that wasn't ordered and in place as a threat to themselves, the Agency, and American "security". They trusted nobody, displayed little emotion and feared most things they didn't understand. It would be a struggle for any of our scientists to explain even the most basic of principles of international cooperation to them; let alone the concept of a guy entering from a parallel world!

Ratton's tone was serious and direct. "Yes, I agree this is unprecedented. If these tests match this guy in Africa, then who the hell is *this* James Holden? And what is his agenda?"

I guessed someone at the CIA had finally tracked down the other James Holden. I lay very still, listening as he continued.

"I'm here at the research center now. We've just found out that he's involved with Matthew Zeiss. He's being tested in their lab." He paused while he listened to the response.

"No, we're not sure if he is aware of the NesCom project; we have no record of them knowing each other before. We're still in the process of evaluation. Zeiss's loyalty has always been unclear, but this link with our Holden may well reveal his true colors." Ratton carefully listened to his superior's response. "Yes, I agree with that sir, we don't want this to develop into a national security issue."

Of course nobody in his department or the CIA knew the real situation. Ratton was simply following the procedures of most national security agencies. But the fact was that Ratton's view of "reality" and Zeiss's were two very different things. With all their advanced technology and know-how, the notion of my descending from a parallel reality was totally beyond their comprehension. I was simply seen as a threat that had to be stopped or even eliminated.

I closed my eyes and breathed slowly. I felt helpless lying there in the lab, while forces of authority conspired around me. But I knew that while still in recovery, I was at least safe for a while.

The next time I awoke it was to the bustle of lab sounds. I had no idea of time, but I could see Zeiss and Morell in the observation bay, along with a couple of technicians checking data.

"It's amazing! This guy got top grades on everything we threw at him. Right up there with some of our top flyers," exclaimed one of the lab assistants.

"You sure?" Morell asked, grabbing the technical printout.

"Yes, in fact, since we did the extra tests, we found the results even more surprising. He seems to have exceptional co-ordination and an incredible mind for detail. Except for some unusually low energy levels, he is the perfect specimen!"

Morell studied the data sheet before turning to Zeiss. "Well, you certainly seem to have trumped us, Matthew. Your Mr. Holden seems to know about our procedures, even our work on fusion energy, yet he's never worked for us. These extra tests confirm everything."

Zeiss took the report and scanned it. "Who authorized these extra tests?"

"We did." Paul Ratton, with two other men, entered the observation bay.

Morell turned to Zeiss and shrugged his shoulders. 'We had no choice, Matthew. It's CIA. I was going to talk to you about it."

Zeiss turned to face Ratton. "What's this all about? I'm Matthew Zeiss, I authorized this evaluation. I'm conducting the research into this individual."

"Yes, doctor, we are aware of your work. However, you've gone as far as you need to regarding this investigation. I'm sure you don't want any negative consequences."

"Meaning what? Are you trying to threaten me? This experiment is not yet complete; this man is still under significant sedation".

Significant sedation? Zeiss must have known that the drugs they'd given me would have worn off by now. As I looked through the observation window I saw him move round, blocking Ratton's view of me. I realized then that Zeiss was deliberately drawing their attention away from me—trying to warn me. I knew that if I were taken by Ratton there would be no escape. I would be caged like an animal and questioned, never able to convince them who I really was.

I lay listening to their conversation knowing I needed to escape from the situation that was unfolding around me.

"Are you really saying that this is the same guy on the networks this morning—this so called mystery man?" Morell enquired.

"We believe so, Mr. Morell."

"What has he done?" Zeiss asked.

"Activities that imply a possible violation of our national security. How else could he have known so much about the operational procedures here, Doctor Zeiss?"

"You think he's a spy?" queried Zeiss.

"If that's what you want to call him, doctor."

"He doesn't seem much like a spy to me," Zeiss replied.

"We're not concerned with your views, doctor. We've checked with our people in Africa. They're very thorough. They confirm that the real James Holden is still there and that he's alive. Whoever you think this man is, he is not James Holden."

I began to loosen the wires attached to my body as they continued their argument. To my right I could see a door that I knew the technicians had exited from earlier. I felt it must lead eventually to a main exit door.

The confrontation in the observation bay was continuing.

"He's still under my jurisdiction, and I need more time with him," Zeiss countered.

"We have the authority to take him now doctor."

"Authority from whom?" Zeiss asked sharply. "This man is in a fragile state. He cannot possibly be moved from this facility today".

I stretched one leg then the other out of the bed. I felt the cold floor beneath my bare feet as I slid off the bed. I was holding my breath to try and be as quiet as possible as Ratton continued asserting his control of the situation.

"You ask whose authority? Our own authority, doctor. Our job is security. It's what we do. We maintain the status quo."

"And what if you're wrong. What if you don't understand what's happening here?"

"Then no one does, doctor." Ratton replied harshly.

Monitor wires swayed erratically around the treatment bed as I grabbed a light grey technician's coat and stepped out of the recovery room.

The corridor outside was empty. I put on the technician's coat and buttoned it up, covering my thin paper gown. About half way down the corridor I passed a doorway marked "Staff Changing". Inside were rows of lockers, but someone had left their clothes piled carelessly on a bench. I pulled on some pants and a T-shirt. The clothes were way too big, but I pulled the laces tight on the sneakers and slipped back out into the corridor, the lab coat pulled over the top. I walked toward an exit sign, passing two security personnel engrossed in conversation. I stood in front of the exit door as a bright security beam swiped the plastic ID badge attached to the pocket of the coat. The door automatically slid open. I found myself standing in a large forecourt. I scanned the area, knowing I had little time before the alarm was raised. I spotted a space capsule exhibited on a concrete foundation next to a boundary fence. Jogging over awkwardly in the ill-fitting shoes I hid behind it, peering back at the main building.

It was then that I heard the sound of a child's voice behind me. "Is that what gets you home, mister?"

Startled, I turned and stared down at a small boy, no older than seven years, pointing toward the capsule.

"Is that what gets you back home?" he said again with an innocent questioning gaze.

My eyes focused on the capsule. I gently placed my hand on its worn charred surface. Moments of the chaotic decent rapidly flashed through my mind. I felt a strange weariness come over me. As though all the turmoil of the past events had suddenly caught up with me and been compounded in that very moment. I looked down at the innocent wonder on the small child's face. "Yeah, son, this is what gets you home."

Within a second a woman's voice called out. "Joey. Time to go!"

The child's mother stood some way off next to a yellow courtesy bus displaying the words City Visitors. I saw other children with their parents boarding the bus. I weighed up my chance. There was no other option. An alarm from the building sounded as I walked with the boy toward the bus and mingled with other parents and children before boarding. I found a seat at the back away from the other families and slumped down, trying to look as inconspicuous as possible.

The bus slowly moved toward an exit gate. A security guard halted the bus at the gate and spoke with the driver. As a phone rang in his security hut, the gate lifted and the bus moved slowly out into the street. I closed my eyes and breathed a sigh of relief.

23

It began to rain as I sat staring out of the bus window. Then it fell harder, blurring the twilight images of people walking the city streets. It reminded me briefly of when I had first arrived here. As the rain dissolved my view, I caught my reflection in the glass window. I looked gaunt and disheveled; weakened by the recent turn of events.

The other passengers seemed to be children with their parents on an educational visit. Families left the bus at different stops and I decided to leave when the young boy and his mother disembarked.

I stood alone on a deserted rain-swept corner, looking upwards, as teeming rain, illuminated by the bright city street lights, splashed hard against my face.

Only the thin lab coat protected me from its driving force.

Through the haze of the rain I noticed a metallic, silver truck parked on the opposite corner. It shimmered, almost like a mirage, as the rain pounded its metallic surface.

"Red Hawk," I mumbled to myself.

I walked toward the truck and peered through its tinted glass passenger window. Silently, the truck door slid open. Red Hawk sat at the driver's wheel looking back at me—as though he'd been waiting for me.

"What are you doing here, Red Hawk?"

"Just wondered how you're getting on, Mr. Holden."

"I'm in one hell of a mess, if you really want to know."

He beckoned me to climb in. "I thought your path would be difficult," he said.

"So you know about all this?"

"Yes."

"How?"

"Because I was meant to."

"Who are you, Red Hawk? Why do you always talk in riddles?"

As Red Hawk looked into my eyes his voice became softer, though with a quiet intensity.

"Your worlds are synchronized, Mr. Holden. They run with a similar parallel resonance. Shifts of great significance are happening in both. Sacred ancient wisdom, once hidden, is beginning to be uncovered. You are being forced to make choices. This wisdom can help you."

"What are you talking about, Red Hawk? I don't need vague mystical words about wisdom. I need to find the right science and technology to get me back."

"It's not easy for you, Mr. Holden. You have been conditioned to think a certain way. But that way does not serve you anymore. You have been given the opportunity to accelerate your development by experiencing this and understanding the freedom of expansion within yourself.

"Since you arrived here, you have learned about ancient teachings and the power of resonance used by ancient cultures, but you chose not to look further at this. Everything around you is vibrating energy, but vibrating at different frequencies. This world is no different.

"You are a human being and therefore have your own resonance. With this energy and using your intention you have the power to create whatever you want and go wherever you desire. There are vibrational reference points for each reality—you don't need technology to find these. You just need to connect with the conscious energy within you and turn within for guidance. Your old ideas of limitation are not actual."

I looked hard into Red Hawk's eyes, trying to comprehend his words.

He continued. "You are entering a new age, an age of 'knowing.' Your old beliefs don't serve you anymore. You will begin to see and understand the very fabric of your reality. Your belief in technology is fine, but it can be a distraction from knowing the true powers that lie within you. Don't be distracted and seduced by the outer planes. It is not more technology you need but technique, technique to develop within yourself.

"The ancients knew this and even had the knowledge and wisdom to
manipulate light and energy into matter. The world you perceive is not solid, but merely a dance of many atoms coming together through your consciousness. It is coming together by you and through you.

"You, as with everyone, are the director of your reality, Mr. Holden, and have within you everything you need. Yes, even the knowledge to get home. You just need to realize this, to move from your old paradigm into the new and seize your power."

A moment of silence ensued before I replied. "I really don't understand these words you speak, Red Hawk."

Red Hawk looked back at me with compassion and smiled gently. "I cannot help you further, Mr. Holden. Perhaps the drama of your final journey will force you to understand."

He hesitated for a brief moment, then continued. "But, I must forewarn you, Mr. Holden."

I looked at Red Hawk with a feeling of apprehension.

"Your own energy will soon weaken and disperse, ultimately to a dangerous level. Two identical energies with the same unique morphic field cannot exist in the same dimension of time and space. Only one can survive. The other will simply fade away or be destroyed. This is a proven scientific fact, Mr. Holden, part of your own modern scientific research."

I sat in silence, gazing back at him trying to comprehend his words.

Then, with tenderness in his voice, "I must leave you now my friend … I wish you well on your path."

These were the final words I heard from Red Hawk. They seemed to amplify and echo within my mind as I slowly closed my weary eyes.

I stood on a deserted, rain-swept street corner, rain splashing hard against my face. I looked over at where Red Hawk's metallic vehicle had stood. The space was empty, as if the space had never been filled, as if I had just experienced a dream or some fleeting figment of my imagination.

I turned and walked toward a telephone booth positioned outside a shabby run-down building named The Falls Hotel. I entered the phone booth and phoned Porter with details of my location. I needed to make contact with Zeiss one more time and knew Suzanne could help. In his serene and efficient manner, Porter said he would contact Suzanne and ask her to meet me at the hotel.

24

Leanchek stepped out from the NASA Control room and greeted Suzanne. She had been waiting patiently, her coat wringing wet from the heavy rain outside.

"Hello, Suzanne, thanks for coming." he said.

"Why am I here?"

"Something unusual has happened."

"What do you mean?"

"We're receiving some transmissions."

She stared questioningly back at him. "Not from …?"

"We don't know what it is or who it is, but we are seeing images on the NVI screen."

"From his node implant?"

"We think so, but we're not sure!"

Suzanne almost crumpled as Leanchek lent his hand in support.

"We're recording the transmissions, trying to enhance the images, but we're really not sure what we're looking at.

We need you to stay, Suzanne, we're going to need your help."

"Yes, yes, of course." she replied—still trying to gather herself.

They both entered the control room. Inside there was a group of people chatting who, upon seeing her, stopped their chatter and quickly left. She moved over to the blank viewscreen and stared at it in silence.

25

I sat alone at a table in the dingy hotel bar. An overweight barman washed beer glasses and eyed me up with some suspicion. I must have looked conspicuous, sitting there in my rain-soaked coat. The bar area was deserted, and the decor had seen better days. I had been sitting there alone for well over an hour, drinking just the one beer. I had found a couple of crumpled up bills in the pocket of the pants I'd stolen, and I had no idea how long they might need to last me.

I peered over at a clock on the wall opposite. It read 8:20 pm.

"Hi!"

I turned and saw Suzanne, her raincoat dripping wet. "I can't stay long." She took it off and sat down next to me. She looked stunningly beautiful; even soaking wet.

"You came." I said.

"You thought I wouldn't? Porter gave me very detailed directions."

Suzanne looked around at the deserted bar area. "How did you find this place?"

"I come here all the time."

She smiled at me as she shook her raincoat.

"We've never had rain like this before."

"Would you like a drink?" I asked.

"Please, red wine."

I signaled to the barman for a glass of red and another beer for myself.

We looked at each other, as if searching for answers to questions we had not yet asked.

"They're looking for you all over, you know that? Clive Dillinger mentioned you on his late night show. He called you the 'mystery man of the desert'."

"Clive Dillinger. Is he famous?"

The barman wandered over, placed a glass of wine and a beer on the table and looked at us both with curiosity before walking back to the bar.

"He hosts just about the biggest network talk show on television."

I smiled back wearily at her "I didn't know that." I cringed slightly as I rubbed the side of my right eye with my forefinger.

Suzanne, aware of my discomfort, moved closer, touching my arm. "You okay? You look terrible."

"Yeah, I'm okay.

There was a moment of silence as our eyes met.

"I'm going to need your help, Suzanne."

"Help?"

"I need you to contact Zeiss. I now know how he can help me."

"How?"

"NesCom."

"What's NesCom?" She replied curiously.

"It's a sort of underground linear accelerator attached to a quantum field oscillator. They call it quantum entanglement."

"They call it what?"

"Well, anyway, Zeiss designed this thing under the desert. I stumbled across some of the research papers when I was at the laboratory for the tests."

"So?" she responded.

"It's designed to teleport matter using morphic resonance-like frequencies. Zeiss has almost cracked it, but ultimately he will need a human being to prove it."

"To prove what?"

A man in a dripping wet coat entered the bar and ordered a shot of whiskey. In a quieter voice, I said, "To prove the existence of other frequencies, other dimensions. It's what Zeiss has been working on all his life. It will be his ultimate achievement."

"And you want to be a part of his experiment?" she replied questioningly.

I moved closer to her. "I can't survive here, Suzanne. He knows that."

"How does he know?"

I looked again with concern at the stranger by the bar, then turned back to Suzanne. "Authorities fear anything they don't understand. Even Zeiss's work could be under threat. They have been trying to sabotage his reputation for years. I just don't have much time here, Suzanne."

"But this experiment is dangerous, isn't it?"

We heard the sound of a glass being placed on the bar table and briefly looked over as the stranger left. I turned back to Suzanne. "Yes, it is dangerous."

She gently placed her hand on mine. I looked down at her hand then back up at her face.

"You know what's happening, don't you?" she said almost whispering.

I nodded gently. There was a silence between us that seemed like eternity.

"I want to be with you, Suzanne. Always. You know that?"

"Then?" she asked, questioningly, as emotion glistened in her eyes.

"I have to go back."

"Why do you keep saying that?"

"You want me to stay?" I asked, hesitantly.

"I want what's right! What's right for us. If this goes wrong everyone will lose. We could go away together. Somewhere!"

There was more silence between us as Suzanne gently caressed the side of my weary aching face.

"I have something I want to give you," I said quietly.

I took out the crystal from my pocket and handed it to her. She took hold of it and caressed its smooth surface.

"It's beautiful — Where did you get it?"

"My wife gave it to me before I left."

"She gave it to you? Where did she get it?"

"From a shaman. She insisted I take it with me."

"A shaman?"

"From Sedona."

She carefully examined the crystal, holding it delicately between her fingers in front of a small candle on the table in front of us. "It has small crystalline triangles within it. Do you know what that means?"

"I have no idea." I replied.

"They say these hold everything in existence — All That Is. This is very special."

I looked at her, trying to comprehend what she was saying. She stared back at me as if some sudden realization had swept over her.

"This wasn't meant for me. I can't accept this."

I was stunned by her sudden rejection. "But I want you to have it, Suzanne."

"You don't understand. This wasn't meant for me. It was given to you for a reason. I don't know why but I know you were meant to have it." She hesitated, her voice now full of emotion. "I have to go now. Zeiss is speaking at the Academy tomorrow. I'll try to arrange a meeting for you at his hotel. It won't be easy—he's surrounded by security."

She stood without looking at me. I felt her mind, tortured with emotion, as she hurriedly grabbed her raincoat and left the bar. I didn't understand at the time what all this was to mean. I only knew that Suzanne had realized something in that moment. Something that I didn't. I just felt numbed and helpless.

I threw what cash I had on the table and moved toward the exit door. The barman looked up from the television.

"Hey, mister, come over here."

I stopped, hesitating, and walked slowly back toward him. He pointed to the television screen.

"Don't you think this guy looks a bit like you?"

I looked at my image displayed on the screen from a live television newscast report. I tried to stay calm. Then, with a sudden rush of inspiration I said, "Everyone wants to look like that guy! That's how you get on the Clive Dillinger show."

It seemed to work. The barman chuckled to himself. I left the bar.

26

In the NASA control room, Suzanne stood close to a view-screen displaying blurred, distorted images of the research center observation room. Leanchek sat at his control desk observing her. She studied the images intensely, trying to comprehend their meaning, then turned to Leanchek. "Is it a hospital?"

"We don't know."

"Where is it coming from?"

"We don't know that either, Suzanne."

"But you designed this thing, didn't you?"

"There is no logic to any of this, Suzanne. We started to receive these images yesterday. We have no trace of the location or from where it's being transmitted."

The screen suddenly blanked out.

"We have more pictures coming through. They're being processed, optimized to enhance the picture quality." Leanchek explained, "It's so we can see more clearly if it's coming from him ... But there are no guarantees, Suzanne!"

27

I sat in silence next to Porter in the Bowen limousine looking over at Zeiss's hotel entrance adjacent to the main academy lecture hall. People filed through showing their passes and invitations to security guards as they entered.

I had returned to the Bowen residence to find it deserted and much of the furniture covered with white sheets. The Bowens had found the limelight they had been thrust into a little unsettling. Being connected with the mystery man of the desert had been just too overwhelming for Debra.

I turned to Porter.

"Rio, eh?"

"Yes, Mrs. Bowen felt it would be best under the circumstances. Her father also has business interests there and personally knows the president. I feel they want to make the emotional distance more permanent, sir," Porter mused.

"You should have been a diplomat, Porter."

He smiled but didn't respond.

Again, there was a brief pause between us, that silence in which you feel comfortable and safe, where nothing needs to be said.

But then, out of that silence, I felt moved to speak. "You've been a good friend to me, you know that, Porter?"

"I only did my job, sir."

"No, you did more than that. You put your job on the line. Not many people would have done that."

Porter smiled but did not reply.

"Did you ever marry?" I asked.

Porter seemed slightly taken aback. "Good heavens, no, at least not in this lifetime. I was close to someone once, a long time ago, but it wasn't to be."

As we stared out of the car window toward the gathering crowds, Porter asked a question that I was not expecting. "Mr. Holden, would you do something for me?"

"Anything." I replied.

"Would you try to find me in your other world, find out who I am and what I'm doing? I would really appreciate that."

I looked back at him, astonished. "You believe me, Porter. You really believe everything I've said?"

"I think I always have. When I saw you and your lady Suzanne talking together on the terrace that evening at the party, I somehow knew. As I watched you something told me you had always known each other and always would."

I looked back at Porter with some emotion.

"Sure, I'll find you, Porter. I promise you that."

Porter took a key from his pocket and handed it to me. "I won't be going back to the house, Mr. Holden. You can use the rear door to get in. Nobody will know you're there."

"Where are you going?"

"The Bowens expect me to join them in Rio, but maybe it is time for me to move on. I'm not sure."

I looked at him, knowing that it was possibly the last time I would see him. Porter had helped me in more ways than I could have imagined. Now I was going to journey on without him. We got out of the limousine and shook hands. Although it felt rather formal, it seemed appropriate and, of course, very Porter.

As I left him I felt the deep emotion of the moment. But, I didn't turn back.

As I walked toward Zeiss's hotel, I passed a crowd of reporters and photographers jostling for the best positions on the academy steps. A young female television reporter was covering the scene live for one of the networks. I tried to catch her report as she spoke to the camera.

"And so the focus is now here at the Academy of Science where Doctor Zeiss will be giving his final lecture. Until now he has refrained from giving any interviews about his dealings with the so-called mystery man whose whereabouts are still unknown."

I looked up at the surrounding buildings and saw an array of security cameras panning the scene. I moved quickly toward the hotel.

Zeiss was sitting at his desk, studying some papers, as I knocked and entered his room. The door was unlocked, and he looked up as if he was expecting me.

"You've become famous, Mr. Holden!" Zeiss pointed over to the television showing the news reports about me.

"We need to talk, doctor—I need your help."

"But you ran away from my help, Mr. Holden, remember?"

"They were ready to take me—you know that."

Zeiss stared at me and gestured to a seat opposite him. "How can I help you?"

"Your science is more advanced than ours. You have made discoveries and developed capabilities which are still unknown to us.

"In some ways we have become more advanced, but not in others. But you still haven't told me how I can help you."

"NesCom"

"You know about this?"

"Yes, the linear accelerator you've built in the desert."

Zeiss stood up and walked to the window, then turned back to me.

"You're very privileged, Mr. Holden. Few people know of this."

"You understand the laws of frequency and resonance. The levels of coherence needed to move energy even within different dimensions of space and time. But, ultimately you're going to need a human to prove your theory. If I can get back, it would prove the existence of other realities for you and everyone."

"You seem to have learned a great deal about my work, Mr. Holden."

"All I know is you're the only person able to do this, the only person able to help me."

Zeiss walked back to his desk and put his glasses on the table. He stared at the television screen, at images of people gathering outside the academy. I sensed that his mind was heavy with responsibility.

"To attempt such an experiment at this stage would be extremely dangerous, Mr. Holden."

"So you do believe me, doctor. Everything I've said?"

"Yes. Nobody else could possibly know what you know. Every single test we did proved that. Your lady Suzanne was also convincing when I spoke with her."

I sat back and gave an outward sigh of relief.

"But how this could have occurred, I'm not sure," he said.

"Could it have been the Arctic laser tests they were experimenting with?"

"Possibly, or that combined with the unusual solar activity you described. It could have caused a massive frequency shift, possibly altering your energy field and creating a coherent vortex. The chance of those events occurring simultaneously is possible, but remote. There may have been another reason."

"Like what? I enquired.

"I'm not sure."

I waited briefly for more analysis, but none came. "So, doctor. What is your decision?"

"We may be more scientifically advanced than your world, Mr. Holden, but my work is highly controversial and still unproven. It would be extremely dangerous to involve a human at this stage. There are very high risks attached."

"I'm aware of that."

"We have had success transferring matter within this dimension, but what you are asking is much more complex. If these calculations are fractionally wrong it could result in the end of your life, Mr. Holden."

I listened to his words, but I knew instinctively what I had to do. Zeiss was my only hope. I had to convince him.

"I can't physically survive here. You know that, doctor. Two identical human energies surviving in the same dimensional field is simply not possible."

"Agreed. Especially if they interact directly with each other. You're a very clever man, Mr. Holden."

"Not really. I was told that by somebody."

Zeiss looked out towards the window, deep in thought.

For a few moments there was complete silence between us. Finally, he turned back to me. "Okay, my friend. But we'll need to work fast. There are many people looking for you. I'll make the arrangements, and get my people to collect you."

I nodded in agreement, slightly stunned by his sudden decision. I told him about the secret door at the rear of the Bowen house and suggested that his people could pick me up from there.

Zeiss picked up a telephone receiver and started to dial a number.

In that moment I felt great compassion toward Zeiss. "Doctor, I really appreciate the risks you're taking on this."

Zeiss put the phone down and stared hard into my eyes. "Whatever happens to me is not important. Everyone chooses their own destiny. We can only search for truth and make it open and transparent. This world is not perfect, Mr. Holden. We have a certain material wealth, but there are still forces out there trying to obstruct knowledge, to dull people's minds and keep them asleep. People who want to maintain power or impose misguided forms of security."

These were the words of a humble man. There was no ego with Zeiss.

28

I sat alone in the Bowen living room staring at the television screen, surrounded by boxes and furniture draped with white sheets. On the screen was national coverage of the events unfolding at the Science Academy. A disc recording of Porter and me, having fun in the city, silently played on a small screen near the patio doors that lead to the rear entrance. It was the filming we had done together, weeks earlier, after a day at the city library. I had left the player running in repeat mode, maybe to remind me again of the good times I had had with Porter. Or maybe just to make me feel less alone.

There was loud applause from the television as Zeiss walked up to the podium to deliver his final speech. He looked down at his notes, hesitated for a moment, then put them in his pocket. I sat silently, staring at the screen.

"Ladies and gentlemen, I have spoken to you at length over these past few days. Today I will be brief and to the point. As a society, we have progressed at lightning speed.

Advanced technology has given us materially much of what we need. We have finally uncovered the knowledge of free energy and fought to make it available, we have been able to produce enough food to feed more in the world. We have sent a manned mission to Mars, and most of our cities are clean and relatively safe. But, my friends, of ourselves and the reality in which we live, we know very little. Even our greatest outward journey is only a small step compared with the inner journey we need to take to know and understand ourselves.

"We are also beginning to discover Noetic science that looks at the very fabric of our consciousness by using intuitive knowing—a knowing that lies deep within us. But these are things we will discuss in detail at a later time. Today, I wish only to make a brief statement.

"Very soon, ladies and gentlemen, I will be able to demonstrate to you living proof of other dimensions of reality, simultaneous realities that are very close to our own. It is now highly probable we all exist in other dimensions of the same time and same space, just at a different resonance and frequency. By discovering these things, we can begin to gain profound knowledge, a deeper understanding of ourselves and the universe we live in. I vow today that this knowledge will be available to all people everywhere. Not concealed or hidden by secret hierarchies of authority and told to only a few. People will be able to decide for themselves the truth, and what paths they will take and beliefs they will have. Gaining a true understanding of this knowledge will be our greatest goal, our greatest quest, and our greatest achievement. Thank you."

Initially there was silence, the audience seemingly stunned by the directness of his speech. Then applause began to swell. Finally, everyone stood in rapturous adulation.

I sat silently watching Zeiss leave the stage before turning and staring out of an open window. The coincidence of my meeting Zeiss and helping him trying to prove his theory was incredible. I'd never believed in synchronicity before, but my thinking about this and many other things was changing.

As I continued to reflect on Zeiss's words, I was suddenly jolted out of my reflective mood by the sound of the telephone ringing. It continued to ring until the voicemail kicked in.

"Hi. It's Jim here. I'm on my way from the airport. What on earth's been going on over here? Okay, I'll see you all soon."

I stared in horror at the machine, realizing I had just heard my own voice. I moved over to the machine and stared down at it as panic began to build inside me.

The telephone rang again. I hesitantly picked up the receiver. Suzanne spoke with agitation and nervousness in her voice. "Jim, Zeiss has told me he's agreed to do this. But it's too dangerous. I don't think you should go ahead."

"Suzanne, listen, something's happened."

"What?"

"I don't have much time. Debra's husband's on his way back."

"Who?"

"Her husband, the geologist. The other James Holden. He was in Africa, remember?"

"How can he be coming back?"

"They must have told him something. Suzanne, stay away from here. It's too dangerous."

The front door bell chimed. In panic, I dropped the phone and pushed myself hard against the wall. The phone whined for a while before going dead.

I heard the sound of a key as it turned in the latch. Then footsteps in the hallway. I edged toward the dimly lit hall and waited by the joining door. Perspiration formed on my forehead as I heard the click of a briefcase opening. Papers shuffled. I hesitantly peered around the door and stared down the hallway.

I saw the back of a man's body as he unpacked a small briefcase on top of the hall table. He seemed to sense my presence. Slowly the man's head turned. In front of me stood the image of the geologist. His hair was longer, different. But, in that moment, I was in no doubt that I was looking at the image of myself.

"Anyone home?" he called out vaguely, looking in my direction.

Then he saw my shadow in the dim hall light.

"Who are you?"

Gripped with fear, I didn't answer.

"Hey, who are you?"

I felt him move toward me, then, abruptly, he stopped as the sound of the front doorbell chimed. It continued resonating with increasing loudness. I peered around the door and saw him walking away toward the front door. As he opened it I saw Suzanne standing in front of him in a bright shimmering light. She looked at him with disbelief. I stood motionless staring along the hallway as the two of them tried to comprehend each other. I saw her collapse to the ground, distraught, and unable to speak. I observed him kneel down and gently help her to her feet to escort her into the house. The geologist supported her as they walked together along the hallway toward the living room.

Suzanne froze in fear as the bewildered geologist entered the living room. His eyes scanned the room for the intruder before resting on the small screen playing the silent images of Porter and me in the city. He looked at the screen, stunned, trying to understand what he was seeing. The patio doors were open, billowing curtains swaying in a gentle breeze. I turned my gaze away and continued my retreat from the house. He would have heard the sound of a car fade off into the distance.

I had escaped, with the turmoil of the experience raging within my mind.

I arrived at Zeiss's experimental accelerator complex, isolated somewhere in the desert. A technician punched a bunch of numbers into a security entry system.

Pristine metal doors slid open. I was escorted into an elevator. The doors closed behind us and we descended to the heart of the underground accelerator complex.

A visor was mounted over my pale, stressed face, as I sat strapped in a silver bullet shaped capsule. Technicians spoke to each other in my headpiece as small screens projected a mass of complex technical information in front of me. I looked at my screen and saw Zeiss in the control room, deep in conversation with his technical staff. Seeing I was watching him, he moved over to the control window and looked down at me. Then I heard his voice in my headpiece.

"I think we're ready, my friend." He continued to stare empathetically at me until the accelerator capsule door finally closed, cutting off my final sight of him.

I heard the hum of the accelerator motor as it started up. Thousands of digital data images flashed onto my control screen as I moved into a darkened tunnel. My visor began to vibrate as the capsule gathered speed. I watched a registration needle moved rapidly toward optimal acceleration. My body began to resonate. Then, suddenly there was a decrease in speed. The capsule slowed and stopped somewhere along the tunnel. On my vision screen I saw confusion in the control room. A man stood confronting Zeiss, armed guards on either side of him. I peered more closely and saw the face of Paul Ratton. One of the guards opened fire at various parts of the equipment. My screen blanked out, and the capsule door slowly began to open.

I released myself from my safety harness, climbed from the capsule and stumbled along the dimly lit tunnel toward an exit door. I pulled it open to find another, smaller tunnel tapering off some way along. I entered the tunnel and staggered along its damp murky rock surface until I reached its end. A sheet of dark grey rock stood in front of me. Perspiration poured through the grime on my forehead as I leaned against the rock face, gasping for breath. I looked back along the dark abyss of the tunnel I had just moved through. I felt weak and exhausted, as though all energy had been sapped from me. Without Zeiss, there was no way back. From a distance I could hear the sound of security sirens echoing along the tunnel walls.

As I stared down in despair, a small glint of light reflected off a tiny crystal stone embedded in the black soil below. I stared down at the reflection, then above to a speck of daylight from a narrow shaft angled above me. I scrambled up the rock and began to claw my way up the narrow, jagged, rocky shaft toward the light. With my hands and face cut and bleeding, I peered bleary-eyed over the top of the shaft exit into a blinding light. In front of me was a hot, shimmering desert. I pulled myself up from the narrow shaft and staggered into deep, drifting sand.

After a few yards, I fell down with exhaustion, the hot sun relentlessly beating down. I heard the sound of helicopters in the distance. I looked up and saw a massive jagged rock formation ascending like a monolith from the sand. I staggered up from the sand and moved toward its cavernous entrance. Finally, I rested my weary head against the cool rock face and peered back at my pursuers. I heard the deafening sound of rotor blades as helicopters landed in a cloud of swirling dust some distance from me.

Ratton climbed out from one of the helicopters and stared over toward me. Zeiss pulled up in a security jeep and walked up next to him. Neither of them spoke or acknowledged each other. More security vehicles and an assortment of TV crews arrived and stood poised some way behind them. All became very still in the shimmering heat. I heard only the whispering sound of the desert wind as they all stared silently at me.

I stood at the cave entrance and felt the energy draining from me. Wearily I turned my head and peered into the dark void of the cavern. As I stared into its darkness I sensed it was a void of unknowing, one I felt compelled to enter. Clenching my fists to try and summon the energy I needed, I stepped into the coolness of the cave. I felt consumed by its silence and darkness as I moved along its narrow passageways. The cool cavern air partly relieved the pain from my throbbing blistered face and hands.

I moved more deeply inside the cave along narrow cavities until I came to a rock face that had a small opening cut into it. I pulled myself through the opening and entered a dust-filled chamber. A thin shaft of sunlight cut through the fine dust highlighting a central area. Shivering with exhaustion, I moved forward into the light and slumped to the ground.

Warm specks of sunlight glistened off my sweat-ridden, bloodstained body as I began to feel my energy fading. I squinted upwards at the chamber walls and saw worn ancient carvings and artifacts embedded in the surface. It was then I remembered Red Hawk. I felt his gentle image radiating within my mind. In desperation I whispered, "Help me, Red Hawk. Please help me." But there was nothing. No voice within telling me how to survive.

As I stared down at the lifeless dust below, a total feeling of surrender consumed my body. Somehow my trembling hand was guided to my blood stained shirt pocket. I took out Suzanne's crystal and held it between my shaking fingers. Then, quite suddenly, it dropped from my hand and was buried into the chamber's fine dust below.

As my hand frantically groped to recover it, a symbol, carved with incredible precision into a worn stone surface was partly revealed. I rapidly brushed the remaining dust away and stared down at it trying to comprehend its significance, trying to recognize where I might have seen it before. It showed a series of concentric rings, each ring becoming finer as they finally converged towards its center. As I retrieved the crystal, a thin shaft of sunlight shone through its triangular crystalline structure illuminating the symbol below. Then, as if guided, I placed the crystal in the center of the symbol.

Complete silence ensued as I watched the strands of multi-hued sunlight reflect across the symbol's time worn surface. Then, the beginnings of a deep vibrational hum occurred. Fine streaks of sunlight flickered rapidly across my face as I heard the sound of my pursuers; their footsteps echoing like distant thunder along the narrow cavern walls. I peered up again at the rock carvings, now animated by erratic streaks of light. The vibration increased as my body merged into a spiraling vortex of blinding light. It was like every atom in my body was fragmenting, the denseness slowly dissipating.

As I traveled down this vortex, blurred, distorted images began to vibrate within the chasms of my mind. Flickering images of my life raced before me. Within milliseconds I saw the choices I had made and the events I had experienced. Opaque mythical shapes appeared and disappeared, some resembling ancient symbols that I had somehow known before. It was like my mind was being stretched to accommodate everything. I could be everywhere—free and without limits.

I observed the fertile slopes of the Sahara and the herds of bison roaming its grassy plains. I saw the great seas of Sirius, with its planets among its huge suns. I saw the crystal pyramids of Atlantis and passed great halls of learning with shimmering columns that stretched high toward an endless infinity. I observed a dense mist of knowledge embracing incredible limitless intelligence. It was like touching the etheric body of the universe while feeling the power and resonance of the connecting stars. All within fragments of time.

I observed both past and present in one single moment. I saw the geologist supporting Suzanne as they watched in astonishment the unfolding drama being played out on the national networks. I saw Suzanne with Leanchek gazing in wonder at the blurred, jumbled images being received on the large control view-screen. I hovered above Zeiss, Ratton and my pursuers as they stared downwards, in bewilderment, at the space where I had been crouched and saw only swirling ripples of dust and the partly embedded crystal. I saw Zeiss gather the crystal and watched his eyes glaze over in wonder as it glistened in the sharp light of the dust-filled chamber. I heard the echo of his thoughts, as he desperately sought to understand what he was experiencing in that moment.

Then, a feeling of being pulled away. A force seemingly guiding me to some pre-ordained destination. A distant bluish, opaque, crystalline grid appeared beyond. I moved toward this grid and felt some subtle force aligning me onto a specific path. I entered this matrix and saw the grid had many layers. A vortex with pulsating triangles of light appeared inter-connected with nodes of pure light radiating from the grid. I moved down through the temporal dimensions of its layers, each seemingly tuned into a specific vibration.

As I moved downwards, life memories flashed instantly before me. I saw my wife, my children and moments in history that had influenced my life, all passing within an instant of time.

I saw the three great leaders slain and halted from continuing their noble work. I saw others in high authority choose war and control to satisfy their desires. I saw the great song poet who inspired generations and the electric string-man creating a thousand echoing sounds. I saw a young senator continue his chimes for justice and the great dance-man continuing to inspire with his innovation. The visionary singers devoting their lives to peace and the great exiled leader inspiring his country and then the world. They were all there before me, like flickering moments that stretched beyond time, spiraling though doorways of inter-connecting dimensions.

As the vibrations increased I was aligned to a specific layer where one node resonated with an incredibly intense light. Slowly, I was drawn toward this light and became immersed in its vast shimmering radiance.

A huge crash vibrated within me as my capsule plunged into the ocean. I heard the sound of gushing water as its outer shell broke back onto the surface. Slowly, I felt the calming waves of the ocean beneath me as I faded out of consciousness.

My eyes slowly opened. I saw the capsule hatch swaying gently above my head. I watched as orderly streams of data flowed from a bank of monitors sited on a control panel. I heard technical chatter relayed through my headpiece. I waited, calmly, observing the array of technical equipment surrounding me. Then I heard the distant sound of helicopters approaching.

I looked upwards, through my crystal clear visor, and watched the hatch door slowly open. I squinted as bright shafts of sunlight hit my eyes. A diver in a wetsuit appeared, silhouetted against the intense light. He pulled back the hatch and beckoned me up. I climbed toward him and into the bright shimmering light.

The old man looked up at me and gently smiled. We sat a few moments in silence. Then he spoke.

"You see, for me, this journey became a sacred journey. Before, I had no knowledge of other realities, other dimensions of time. I knew nothing of the unseen subtle world around me. Of course, Red Hawk and the ancients had always known of this. He was both my guardian angel and guide. Maybe that's why he drove me to the City of Angels. Their knowledge of sacred doorways and other parallel realities had been passed down through many generations, but they were special.

"Real understanding comes through inner knowing. Yes, we do have the power to experience and create whatever we want, but we have to connect with this knowing and discover this knowledge.

"The treatment I was given after my return was because the medical profession knew no different. They had no comprehension of what I was telling them. They were simply trying to help me in the only way they knew. But they were living in the old paradigm, feeding me drugs they thought were for my good. Not realizing that, for me, everything had changed.

"The authorities of the day later came up with all kinds of creative theories about what NASA said they had seen on their screens and monitors, explaining it as crossed signals and technological malfunctions. It was only Suzanne who really understood what was happening. These events were never shared because they were deemed not to be in the public interest. That's why I'm telling you this story."

There was a final moment of silence between us, as I sat reflecting on his words. Then, I turned toward the portly barman, engrossed in a television program behind the bar. I walked over toward him, trying to attract his attention to pay for our drinks. Then, I remembered a question I wanted to ask. What of his friend Porter? Did he ever find him? As I turned back I saw the old man was no longer there. It was as though the space he occupied no longer existed. As I walked back I noticed a small crystal on the table where I was sitting. I picked it up and held it between my fingers.

As I studied the crystal, small beams of early morning sunlight glistened off its smooth translucent surface from the small window above. For a moment I was transfixed by its presence and stillness. Then, slowly, my mind drifted off into a place beyond. Beyond his story, beyond his journey, to a place of knowing where I began—just began—to understand.

For book-notes please go to the website:
www.theparadigmshift.com/book-notes

About the Author

Since leaving the London Film School in the mid-seventies David has worked mainly as a freelance director, producer, teacher and more recently as a writer.

Other life experiences have included: teaching in Saudi Arabia, a freelance photographer and drama teacher in London, directing a music promo in *Findhorn*, working in a tin mine in Australia and most famously, singing for forty minutes with Otis Redding in a mini cab!

The Paradigm Shift was initially conceived in a dream and originally written by David as a screenplay, which evolved over many years. Strangely, the dream was also instructing him to get the story made into a feature film.

The book was subsequently written to get the story out to a wider audience and to stimulate interest from inspired visionary producers or like-minded individuals who think the project worthy.

David is presently working on his second novel and is committed to developing the screen version of the dream!

David lives with his wife Linda near Cambridge, England and has two children.

Those interested in the project or who wish to view the booknotes, please visit:

www.theparadigmshift.com

Acknowledgments

I would like to thank all friends
who have supported me on this journey.

To Lesley Payne my US editor, Madeleine Forbes,
who also gave invaluable editorial assistance,
and to Philip Marks who reviewed the science
and provided advice.

Above all, I would like to thank my loving wife Linda
and children Matthew and Suzanne
who have given me unswerving support throughout.

Lightning Source UK Ltd.
Milton Keynes UK
UKOW04f0719081215

264282UK00001B/41/P